# The House of Shells

# of Shells

Andy Monk

*When the long day goes by*
*And I do not see your face,*
*The old wild, restless sorrow*
*Steals from its hiding place.*

*My day is barren and broken,*
*Bereft of light and song,*
*A sea beach bleak and windy*
*That moans the whole day long.*

*To the empty beach at ebb tide,*
*Bare with its rocks and scars,*
*Come back like the sea with singing,*
*And light of a million stars.*

Ebb Tide
Sara Teasdale

# One

The old cottage was perfect for pretty much any illicit activity Jack could think of. There were no onlookers, no prying eyes, no one to see anything that shouldn't be happening.

They'd been no signs of human life, or even of the twentieth century, since they'd turned off the hedge-encased B-road to trundle and bump down the rutted leaf-carpeted lane leading to the House of Shells.

He wasn't planning on burying bodies out here, but he liked the seclusion immediately. He'd been a city boy all his life and had no great love for places littered with unnecessary trees. However, the thought of being alone with Moira in this place, with nothing to break the silence but the occasional gull wheeling overhead and the distant drumming of the surf, excited him in a way he hadn't anticipated. All his reservations about the long drive and the fact they could have just booked a hotel closer to London melted away. There was no need to look over his shoulder and worry who might see them together. Absolutely *nobody* was going to see them here.

Jack climbed out of the car and let the wind assault his dark thinning hair. He glanced over the roof of the Cortina at Moira, who grinned back before rushing down the little path

1

towards the cottage.

"I'm just fine with the bags, don't worry!"

She looked back over her shoulder and stuck out her tongue before disappearing inside.

Jack shrugged and wondered if he should make more of an effort parking the car. The lane, which was little more than a couple of sandy mulch encrusted ruts either side of a strip of grass, continued after the House of Shells to who knew where.

However, it didn't look like the kind of place that suffered much passing traffic.

To his left, beyond a thin scattering of trees and gorse, were a series of undulating dunes crowned with grey-green tufts of marram grass. According to Moira they were known locally as The Burrows. To his right, beyond the house, the land rose sharply, the slopes dense with brambles, oak and whitebeam. The cottage itself was half lost behind wild rose bushes and creeping ivy. Two small windows, one upstairs, one downstairs, peered out towards the dunes. It was the only building as far as he could see in any direction.

Despite his grumbling, there wasn't much in the way of baggage to haul inside. They'd be staying for three nights and Moira had only brought a duffel which he threw over his shoulder. He locked the car out of habit and scooped up his own over-sized sports bag before hurrying inside. There were some groceries they'd picked up in the last sizeable town before they'd hit the coast, but they could wait. He had more pressing concerns.

It had been unseasonably mild in London and blue skies had followed them most of the way down to the sea. As soon as they'd spied the coast, however, rapidly darkening clouds had billowed up from nowhere, thickening quickly into colossal banks of grey stretching from horizon to horizon. Jack's light canvas jacket billowed around him, and, for the first time in months, he felt cold.

Moira had left the door ajar and he shouldered it open, dumping the bags inside. It opened directly into an unfussy living room looking out on the cottage's tangled rose bushes towards the dune field.

"Isn't it perfectly beautiful?" Moira asked, spinning slowly around.

"Absolutely..." Jack muttered, more interested in the way the dark denim of her jeans framed her perfectly beautiful arse.

*Three nights...*

He was peripherally aware of the room around them. It was dominated by a huge old brown sofa that was so battered it would either be ridiculously comfortable or impale an unwary buttock on a broken spring. There was a sun-faded blue rug and roughly stripped floorboards, a TV in a faux walnut case that he doubted would be colour if it could receive any picture at all. Shelves and cabinets were adorned with dog-eared paperbacks interspersed with seashells of all imaginable varieties while the walls held small framed pencil sketches of more seashells. Most of all, however, he noticed the stairs.

Moira pressed her nose against the window and smiled. He slipped a hand around her waist and perched his chin on her shoulder.

"Shall we check out the bedroom?"

"Don't you want to see the kitchen first?"

"No."

"Or the bathroom?"

"Nope."

"But there's an inside toilet and a shower?"

"Not interested."

"You should look around. It's only polite. The house likes you." Moira was prone to come out with such utterances from time to time; the kind that might suggest she was slightly bonkers if you didn't know better.

"I like the house too. We should definitely pay our respects to the bedroom."

"Why the hurry to get upstairs?" She pushed her backside into his groin a little, "Ah-ha, I see…"

"Well, it's been a long drive. I've had to keep my hands on the wheel. Safety first and all."

She twisted around and slung her arms over his shoulders, her misty-grey eyes widening as she raised her chin. It was a look that generally got him to agree to anything.

"We've got all night for that, we should go for a walk, it'll be dark in a few hours."

"I didn't come to this remote, windswept little beauty spot for long romantic walks on the beach, you know?"

"No?" Moira frowned, "then why did you?"

"So I could have four days and three nights unrestricted access to all your beauty spots. Which, frankly, are far more outstanding."

She smiled, stretched up and brushed her lips against his, "Walk first, then sex."

He kissed her back in the hope his lips, not to mention his hopeful erection, might make her see sense, but she squirmed out of his grasp with a giggle and backed towards the door.

"Walk first… if all you wanted to do was stay in bed, we could have just gone to a hotel in Croydon.

Actually, that had been his first choice, but Moira had wanted to do the whole romantic break thing and when the opportunity unexpectedly arose he'd jumped at the chance. Admittedly, the idea hadn't seemed quite so enticing when he'd had to climb out of bed at four in the morning to collect her from her bedsit, but now they were here…

"It's too magical and beautiful to stay indoors!"

He peered out at the darkening sky, but before he could suggest she was too beautiful for him to want to go outdoors, Moira's eyes dropped to the bags,

"Where's the food?"

"In the car."

"Jack! The milk and stuff need to go in the fridge! Sort it out and catch me up, I'll be on the beach getting London out of my hair," she opened the door and slipped outside. Jack hurried after her.

"Hey," he called out, "I thought we were supposed to be spending time together?"

"We are," she spun around and walked backwards, zipping up her battered leather bomber jacket, long black hair whipping about her round elven face, "so be quick!"

"Okay, just don't run off too far."

"Oh, you gonna have to move fast to catch me, old man!"

"I have to catch you now, huh?"

5

"Yep. And if you can catch me, you can have me!" She started running towards the dunes, her laughter dancing in the wind behind her.

Jack swore as he fumbled and dropped the car keys in his hurry to get them out of his pocket.

By the time he'd grabbed the carriers from the car Moira had disappeared from view and he hurried back inside with their shopping, which consisted only of the essentials needed for a short break in a remote cottage, like bacon, bread and beer.

The kitchen was small and functional, it wasn't going to win any prizes for modern living, but it felt warm and homely. Between the heavy wooden cupboards and scuffed worktops more pictures of shells decorated walls painted a deep turquoise. The flagstones beneath his feet felt timeworn smooth. The window over the large Belfast sink, which was cobwebbed with tiny cracks, looked out on a garden even more overgrown than the one in the front and hedged in by the woods clinging to the hillside rising above the cottage.

He threw the groceries onto a round table hidden beneath a red and white checked tablecloth hanging to the floor, before stuffing the perishables into a fridge that hummed and vibrated like an enthusiastic sex toy.

Slamming the fridge door shut he straightened up and was about to rush out after Moira when he heard a giggle in his ear. Flirtatious and playful.

Jack jumped then grinned as he turned, expecting to find Moira in the doorway, twisting a strand of hair between her fingers as she stared up at him with expectant, mischievous eyes.

"Decided against a walk then..."

The kitchen was empty.

Jack hurried back to the living room. The front door was still open, swinging back and forth at the whim of the wind, but it was as empty as the kitchen.

"Moira!"

No answer.

A few hours out of London and he was already hearing things. The floorboards creaked as he crossed the room. If Moira had been behind him and then run off, he would have heard her. The House of Shells wasn't built for sneaking.

Jack slammed the door behind him and headed towards the beach, eager to hear Moira's laughter for real.

\*

The beach was deserted. Which wasn't a surprise given the ripping wind and ominous clouds. The holiday season was over and the locals were probably far too sensible to risk being caught out in the weather. Even a devout indoors man like Jack could tell rain was coming. Shame it hadn't turned up a bit earlier, a serious downpour might have succeeded where his charm had failed and persuaded Moira the sensible place to be was in bed.

As he turned into the biting wind he realised, not for the first time in recent months, he hadn't been thinking primarily with his brain. He had a parka in the boot of the car and a thick Arran jumper in his bag. Both were far more suitable than the light jacket and sweater he'd driven down in.

He'd followed a path of weather-cracked wooden planks, mostly submerged beneath the white powdery sand, through the dunes and onto the beach proper. Once out of the lee of the dunes the wind was cuttingly fierce. Beyond the expanse of wet sand and rippling grey pools the retreating tide had left behind, brigades of horse-tailed waves were being whipped towards the beach in a constant roar.

Squinting against the wind he turned slowly through 360 degrees.

There was no sign of Moira or anybody else.

The beach stretched half a mile or so in either direction and at low tide the sea was a good ten-minute walk across the sands. If Moira had been on the beach, he'd have seen her dark blue jeans and ancient black leather jacket, stark against the wet sand. So she must be in the dunes, playing games.

He smiled, despite the cold. Very occasionally her child-like frivolity irritated him, but he usually found it enormously endearing. There was an infectious charm to it, especially after years of skirting around Amanda's dour silences and humour bypass.

"Coming to get you!" Jack shouted at the dunes rolling along the length of the beach. He glanced over his shoulder just in case he'd somehow managed to miss a cunningly camouflaged dog walker.

There was no dog walker and no reply, just the pounding of distant surf, the cries of gulls and the wind assaulting his ears. He trudged up the nearest dune in the hope of catching sight of Moira; they hadn't seemed particularly high from a distance, but he was soon panting as the dry sand crumbled beneath his boots. His calf muscles were burning by the time he reached the marram grass at the top.

"Shit…"

*How'd I get so old and crap?*

He would have bounded up the dune slope a few years ago and barely been out of breath. But his only exercise for years had been squeezing in a cheeky pint or two on the way home from work, which involved a two-hundred-yard diversion between the tube station and his semi-detached slice of suburban bliss. At least, until Moira came along anyway.

They'd met in a second-hand bookshop on Charing Cross Road, which he'd dived into to avoid a summer thunderstorm. He'd thought her some pretty, arty student who would have an equally arty boyfriend in tow somewhere. He'd also assumed she wouldn't even notice a balding, forty-something pretending to be interested in German avant-garde photography.

He didn't make a habit of openly staring at attractive young women. Honestly. But something about Moira kept dragging his eyes back to her no matter how sternly he lectured himself he was behaving like a lecherous old goat.

When she'd raised her big grey eyes, framed in thick black eyeliner, from the book she was skimming, he'd felt his face flush like a teenager and looked sharply away.

He'd always had great difficulty in guessing what a woman thought when she noticed him. It usually boiled down to a choice between *Oh, he looks rather nice*, or *why is that creepy guy staring at my chest?* It was a life skill he'd never entirely mastered, which was probably why so many nights out during his single days had concluded with nothing racier than a cheese and pickle sandwich and falling asleep on the sofa.

Deciding she was far too young and pretty to be of the former mindset, and he was far too married anyway, he'd shuffled off towards the science fiction section where the danger of distractingly lovely looking girls was substantially less.

However, she'd followed him and instead of giving him a piece of her mind, much to his surprise she'd asked him if he'd like to buy her a drink. She'd looked up at him while he'd fumbled for an answer, cocking an eyebrow when one hadn't been immediately forthcoming, while fiddling with her hair, which was as black as soot and fell past her shoulders.

He'd looked out at the rain dancing on the empty pavements and mumbled something about waiting for the downpour to stop while trying to work out if someone was playing a practical joke on him. Moira had giggled, a deep, throaty noise he'd come to know so well over the following months, shaken her head and taken his hand.

"No, right now," she'd grinned and led him back out on to Charring Cross Road. It had been a thirty-second sprint to the nearest pub; which had been long enough for them both to get soaked to the skin.

He'd spent the next two hours entranced by her every word and movement as he'd sipped warm beer and slowly dried out. She was twenty-three, did something vaguely connected to advertising that didn't pay very much and lived in a bedsit in Fulham. Why on Earth she'd wanted to spend an afternoon in the company of a man nearly twenty years her senior with a receding hairline, a slight paunch and a ring on his finger he couldn't imagine. But she excited him in a way he'd entirely forgotten about for years. Maybe decades.

Two weeks later they'd made love in a hotel room washed by the light of a blinking neon sign outside. Moira had reverentially placed a little cassette player on the bedside table and they'd been serenaded by *The Clash*, who, to Jack's ears, made a terrible racket. Though not as much of a racket as the torturously creaking bed.

They'd finally fallen into spent and exhausted sleep only to be awoken at six AM by the only slightly less musical noise of a pneumatic drill as workman repaired a burst water main. He couldn't remember a happier night in all his life. He'd expected to be racked by remorse and guilt, but the only price he'd had to pay was the inability to get Joe Strummer screaming *White Riot* out of his head for the following fortnight.

And now he was going to have three whole nights with Moira. One after the other...

"Moira!"

If he ever found her again, of course.

He picked his way through clumps of marram grass being tossed into a frenetic dance by the wind; the cloud out to sea was darkening to the ugly purple-black of a boxer's bruise.

"C'mon, it's going to piss down! Let's go back!"

The only reply came from a couple of screaming gulls struggling with the fierce gusts coming off the sea. He could imagine Moira curled up behind a dune, trying to stifle her laughter as he frantically laboured through the sand. He couldn't quite see the joke, but her sense of humour did lean towards the warped at times.

Much like her taste in men he supposed.

A raindrop, fat and cold, hit his face. Did she have some

fetish about getting him soaked to the skin?

"It's starting to rain!" He shouted, rather unnecessarily, as raindrops thudded onto the dry sand, leaving small dark stains where they fell. The wind was increasing to a howling gale too, the scent of the sea ripe upon its furious breath.

He wondered whether she'd circled back to the House of Shells and was flicking through the dog-eared paperbacks on the shelves while cradling a mug of tea. No doubt she'd enjoy a good old chuckle when he eventually squelched across the threshold.

"Ok, I'm going back now!" He shouted again, the words ripped from his mouth by the wind.

Twisting around to face inland he could see the chimney of the House of Shells above the dunes. He'd come further than he'd thought as he retraced his footprints across the sand. It struck him there weren't any other footprints up here. He supposed the wind and rain would smooth them out of the fine dry sand fairly quickly, but it didn't look as if anyone else had come this way for a while. Moira included.

*Guess I wasn't cut out to track anything much.*

If Moira was up here she must have gone in an entirely different direction; hopefully, a direction leading back to bed, where she was now waiting for him wearing nothing but her faded Ramones t-shirt and a mischievous grin.

Maybe halfway back across the dunes, with a trickle of sweat on the back of his neck despite the chill wind ripping about him, Jack stopped and looked up.

*Was that shouting?*

He frowned. Maybe it was a gull in the distance, or kids playing somewhere out of sight. But it had sounded like a voice. Like Moira's voice?

The rain was starting to fall harder, speckling the dry sand and stinging his face. He headed towards the house in a shuffling run before the voice came again, the words lost to the wind howling in from the churning, anguished sea.

"Moira!"

He turned his back to the wind and squalling rain in order to squint up at the dune, which seemed to be higher than any of the others stretched out along the beach. All he could see was marram grass being tossed back and forth by the breaking storm.

"C'mon!" he threw his arms open and tried not to show the irritation that was beginning to gnaw at him, "This is getting stupid!"

The heavens were about to open and she was arsing about playing hide and seek. As if to reinforce his fears, thunder rolled in from the sea. The sky above the waves was a biblical black, save for a thin band of lighter cloud on the very horizon which was partly obscured by hazy sheets of rain. As he watched, lightning split the darkness and a few seconds later another roll of thunder crashed onto the beach.

"Ok, that's enough!" Jack shouted up the dune, "Back to the house, now!"

When no response came, he shook his head and begun running through the dunes, his feet splitting the thin crust of wet sand and sinking ankle deep with each stride. He stumbled a couple of times but managed to keep his balance.

By the time he found the cracked wooden boards cutting through the dunes back towards the House of Shells, his

13

boots were full of sand and the rain streamed down his face.

Jack glanced back up the dune slope. For a moment he thought he saw someone at the summit of that big mountain of a dune in the middle, looking out to sea as the wind whipped long dark hair about them. Then another lightning flash made him blink and when his vision had cleared the figure was gone.

"Crazy girl..."

He sprinted back down the boardwalk as a thunderclap broke about him with a deafening roar. By the time he crashed through the front door of the House of Shells he was sodden, panting and shivering.

It wasn't quite how he'd anticipated things would go. During the long drive from London all he'd wanted to do was look at Moira and reach over to touch her, neither of which were activities recommended in the Highway Code.

Although it was still a while to sunset the house was gloomy under the mountain of black cloud now squatting overhead. Jack found a light switch and the unadorned bulb appeared to consider matters for a bit, before dusting a pale and unwelcoming yellow light on to the shadowy corners of the room.

A pile of thin towels sat in a cupboard outside the bathroom and he used one to dry himself after kicking off his damp clothes. He threw the wet things over the back of a kitchen chair and pulled on clean jeans and a sweater from his bag. He flattened his thinning hair down and blew a long exasperated sigh.

The rain was being thrown against the window. He pulled the curtains jerkily across after a quick glance to see if Moira was running back to the house. She wasn't.

She couldn't still be out on The Burrows, surely? No matter how much someone liked rain, there came a point when the cold, wet discomfort of it eroded the fun. Or maybe he was just strange.

A slow extended creak filtered down from upstairs.

He raised his eyes to the ceiling, which was off-white and uneven. Faded water stains bloomed in a couple of the corners. A grin spread across his face.

Perhaps the rain hadn't held any appeal for her after all. He wasn't entirely sure he'd seen or heard her in the dunes. Perhaps she was up in the bedroom, after all, just wearing *the Ramones* t-shirt she liked to sleep in.

"Moira?"

No reply but the rain rapping on the windows.

The stairs were narrow and steep and Jack bounded up them two at a time; his earlier irritation at Moira's games evaporating at the thought of *The Ramones*.

There were two bedrooms, one back, one front, both resplendent with collections of shells, sun-bleached driftwood, a few old black and white photographs and large double beds; neither of which were adorned with a pretty young woman draping herself alluringly for his pleasure.

Grey half-light filtered through the net curtains in both rooms. Jack didn't bother either drawing the curtains or turning on the lights. Instead, he slumped onto the bed in the front bedroom. The mattress was deep and soft, although the brass frame squealed in protest at his presence.

Jack hoisted his legs onto the bed and shuffled over. Despite being spotless the house smelt faintly of musty disuse, as if he and Moira were the first to cross its threshold in years. The sheets, however, were fresh and welcoming in the way clean linen always was to a tired body.

Maybe a nap wouldn't be a bad idea. He was pissed Moira had run off and was, even more, pissed she hadn't come back yet. He knew he could sometimes be sharp and off-hand when he was in that kind of mood. He hadn't exchanged a cross word with Moira since he'd met her and he really didn't want that to ever change.

She'd come back when she was good and ready. When she'd finished communing with nature or whatever the hell daft ideas young people had these days.

Jack looked around the room, but there was nothing to be seen in the wet, murky light unless you had a fascination for seashells. Instead, he let his eyes close. It had been a long day and, hopefully, when Moira got back it would be a long night too. He let the wind's howl and the rain's beat serenade him and was snoring in minutes.

# Two

Jack awoke with a start.

He'd been shaken by insistent hands and he sat bolt upright in bed, blinking at the darkened room.

"Moira..." he croaked, "...what's wrong?"

When no answer came, he reached out and patted the bed next to him. Empty.

He hadn't drawn the curtains and unfamiliar shadows loitered around the room, but there was no sound bar the rain.

"Hello?"

He peered into the darkness, nothing moved, no sounds came. There wasn't anything to suggest someone else was in the room. Save where his arm still tingled from being shaken.

"Moira, this isn't funny."

Again, nothing but the drumming rain replied.

Jack glanced at his watch, his eyes taking a few seconds to resolve and decipher the glowing dial. It was gone eleven. Moira must be back by now, and still playing games.

Jack fumbled in the darkness for the ancient metal reading lamp he remembered being on the bedside table. When he eventually found it, the switch clicked loudly but to no discernible effect.

He hoped it was just the bulb or fuse. If the house was on a meter, he'd be groping around for hours to find it. The wind howled outside, rattling the window frame. Of course, the storm might have brought power lines down. Great.

Wearily he swung his legs off the bed. A shadow floated in the far corner where the night's meagre light didn't quite seem to reach. It looked for all the world like a figure, small and slight, but a figure all the same. Jack remembered the tingling sensation on his arm again

It had to be Moira.

"Moira…"

Or nothing at all.

The shadow didn't move. He instantly felt embarrassed by the way his heart had started to pound like a little boy afraid of a ghoul at the end of his bed. Jack started to feel his way across the room towards the light switch, edging backwards, keeping an eye on the shadow. Was it moving now? A step forward for every step he took back?

"Very funny, Moira."

The shadow had no form or substance, just uniform darkness. A deeper black against the night. If someone was there, shouldn't the shape change a little as they moved? So, it *was* just a shadow; a coat over a hook or something.

Jack reached out behind him and patted the wall. For some reason beyond the old primal fear of the dark, he really didn't want to turn his back on that shadow.

He found the rocker switch and clicked it over, expecting nothing to happen. Instead, he winced as light flooded the room. He supposed it was as dull and subdued as the downstairs one had been, but to his night sensitive eyes, it seemed like a new sun exploding in the sky. Even through watery squinting eyes, however, it was clear the bedroom was quite empty.

Jack leaned against the door and let his eyes adjust. When he'd finally stopped squinting, he tried to figure out what the shadow had been. There was nothing but a simple hard-backed chair in that corner, the kind he'd probably have used to toss his clothes over if he'd bothered to undress earlier. Nothing else.

He'd been half asleep and had dreamt of been woken by a hand shaking him. The dream must have followed him to wakefulness.

That didn't explain where Moira was, though. Perhaps she'd found him asleep and hadn't wanted to disturb him. Didn't sound much like her, but she could have fallen asleep in front of the TV or after making herself supper. She might even have curled up in the other bedroom for reasons best known to herself.

Jack tried to recall if he'd done anything to upset her, but nothing came immediately to mind. Not that Moira had ever been particularly moody. Unlike Amanda, who'd stomped off to quarantine herself in the spare room in response to any number of his misdemeanours over the years.

She'd seemed fine during the drive down, bright-eyed, excited and almost crackling with happiness.

Still rubbing the sleep from his eyes, he wandered out onto the landing.

Someone laughed.

The same laughter he'd heard in the kitchen earlier. Distant, playful, girlish. Jack whirled around and stared into the bedroom. Unless Moira was hiding under the bed or was in the old mahogany wardrobe, the laughter hadn't come from the bedroom. Even though it sounded like it had.

Just the wind. Obviously.

The back bedroom was empty and Jack descended the stairs into darkness. More little paintings of seashells lined the wall; cockles, razor clams, whelks, periwinkles, mussels, oysters, goose barnacles. Somebody liked their shells.

Enough light escaped from upstairs for him to find the downstairs light switch.

The couch was empty save for a few bright mosaic cushions; it didn't take long to confirm the rest of the downstairs was empty too. The House of Shells wasn't a big place.

Jack went to the window at the front, pulled back the net curtain and peered out into the darkness. The rain was still falling heavily, though the thunderstorm seemed to have passed. The wind had abated a little.

For the first time since Moira had run off laughing into The Burrows, he stopped feeling pissed and started feeling worried.

There was no good reason for her not to have found her way back to the cottage by now. There was no village nearby, no pub for her to find shelter from the storm in. It'd been gloomy and overcast, but it'd still been light when he'd headed back. She couldn't have gotten lost! All she needed to do was walk along the beach and find the boardwalk path cutting through a low point in the dunes and follow it back to the House of Shells.

Something must have happened.

If he *had* seen her atop that dune in the middle of a thunderstorm...

"Oh shit..."

How close had the lightening been? What did they say? One second for every mile between the flash and the bang? The lightning must have still been a way off, but Jack didn't know enough about storms to work out how likely a lightning strike on top of that dune was. In fact, all he knew about storms was it was a damn stupid idea to be loitering in the middle of one.

An image flashed into Jack's head; Moira's battered red baseball boots, singed, blackened and smouldering in the sand.

Jack ran upstairs and checked under the bed and in the old mahogany veneer wardrobe. He found only dust balls under one and cheap metal hangers in the other.

It didn't seem likely Moira would be hiding in the cottage, but he was prepared to grasp any straw other than the thought she might be lying dead and burnt to a crisp atop The Burrows. What should he do?

There was a diarrhoea brown phone in the front room. Should he call the police? An ambulance?

And say what?

*My girlfriend went out for a walk and hasn't come back. I think she might have been hit by lightning as she pranced about on a big sand dune in the middle of a storm.*

Didn't you need to wait 24 hours before reporting a missing person? An adult anyway. And the ambulance service would need, at the very least, a body.

He left the phone. Instead, Jack pulled his boots on and

21

hurried back out into the rain. From the boot of the Cortina, he pulled out his parka and a torch Amanda had bought him a couple of birthdays ago.

It was square and yellow. In addition to the main torch, it had an orange flashing hazard light on the top. It also had black plastic handles that could twist round to form a stand to place it on the road if you broke down.

In truth, Amanda had never been great when it came to presents.

He twisted the handles so he could hold the torch like a lantern. He'd never had cause to use it in anger. It'd sat half-forgotten in the boot of his car in case he broke down somewhere dark and remote. The beam was more powerful than he expected, cutting the night and illuminating the rain slashing out of the featureless black sky.

Jack tugged the hood of his coat up and hurried back into The Burrows.

# Three

*"Moira!"*

Jack shouted her name as he ran along the boardwalk. The wood was slick and slippery from the incessant rain, the sandy puddles between the slats sloshing beneath his tread.

The boardwalk had been easy to find, the dune where, he thought, he'd seen Moira was harder. The torch beam picked out the marram grass tossing in the wind atop the dunes, but, spotlighted from below, each fragment of illuminated dune looked much like another.

He kept shouting, tasting the cold, salt-tainted, rain on his lips as he threw back his head. He heard nothing but the pound and roar of the surf in return, louder than before as the tide had crept up the beach towards the foot of The Burrows.

*Why am I shouting?*

If Moira were close enough or alive enough to reply she wouldn't be sitting in a dune field, she'd be back in the cottage. With him. In bed. Jack tried to shut down that thought and the gnawing fear it provoked.

When he'd gone about halfway to the beach, by his own shaky reckoning at least, he stopped and carefully swept the torch beam back and forth. He thought this was the spot where he'd come down the dune earlier, but in the wet, squalling dark he couldn't be sure.

He made out a series of depressions that might have been the remnants of his own earlier footprints. Doubting anything better was going to snag his memory, Jack left the boardwalk and begun to trudge up the slope of the dune.

The rain was falling heavily again. There was still enough wind to hurl it into his face and he had to lean forward to keep his balance and plough up the wet slope. He passed only clumps of marram grass as he followed the bobbing, dancing path the torch sheared through the night.

He was sweating by the time he reached the crest of the first dune. He was almost grateful when the hood of his parka blew back, allowing the rain to cool his face. He'd never understood why some people did this kind of thing for fun. Hauling their arses over hills and mountains, through snow and sand, freezing, boiling, drowning in some far-flung best-forgotten corner of the globe.

Holding the yellow box of the torch in both hands he swung it slowly around, catching the marram grass dancing wildly and casting demented shadow puppets against the higher dunes. There was nothing to see but sand, grass and rain. However, he was pretty sure he recognised the big dune he'd been looking for. In the darkness it rose above him, the grass upon it seemingly whipped even harder by the wind. It was almost as if the dune were alive, the grass erupting from the sand in writhing, undulating clumps of unremitting tortured movement.

Did he really want to go up that dune?

Stupid question. Of course he didn't. But if Moira was up there...

Moira was probably half drunk in a pub, flirting with some burly fisherman half his age and laughing riotously at his expense.

If she hadn't been sleeping with him so enthusiastically for the last three months, he might have thought she'd just egged him on to get a lift down here. This was her neck of the woods, wasn't it? She'd intimated as much without really telling him anything. She'd certainly known the route down from London well enough. However, she'd always been vague when he asked about her family and he'd never pressed her about it. She was barely more than a teenager and you could go through all kinds of angst with your parents at that age.

He started towards the big dune and tried not to think how much it looked like the haunch of some gigantic beast curled up against the rain, its patchy fur ruffled by the wind.

It was just grass. Grass and sand. Nothing else.

The torch beam bounced madly as he climbed the natural path winding around thickets of marram grass. And it felt like a climb. Had it been this big earlier? Of course it had, but in the darkness it seemed huge.

Jack tried to fix on the light. He was used to darkness being tinged orange with streetlamps, but here, out on The Burrows, the darkness was black and absolute. Other than his torch there were no other lights to be seen, not even from a ship being tossed about out on the ocean.

He knew this place was remote, but surely he should be able to see something else? Especially given the vantage point his leg sapping ascent of Mount Dune gave him. A village? A house? A pub where all the locals would stop talking to peer curiously at you if you ventured inside?

Something?

His chest was tightening and his saliva was starting to taste coppery. He should take up squash again. He should be able to walk up a couple of dunes without risking a coronary. Not as if forty-one was that old.

Maybe he'd face plant into the wet sand to be found by some dog walker (it was usually dog-walkers that found bodies) in the morning. Would there be much of a fuss? *Promising London Architect Found Dead in Mysterious Circumstances*. Well, *Promising* might be stretching it a bit, but *Bored* or *Disillusioned* wouldn't make such good copy. The mysterious circumstances would be why he'd been tramping up a ruddy great sandy hill rather than being at the Designing the Future conference in Swindon, which was where Amanda thought he was.

Of course, there was no conference called *Designing the Future*, in Swindon or anywhere else as far as Jack knew. Though right now he'd be prepared to give away a considerable chunk of money to have persuaded Moira a couple of nights in Swindon would have been far more exhilarating than the House of Shells and this deserted beach.

He bent over and spat into the sand, watching the spittle wash away in a rivulet of rainwater running down the dune.

A lot more bloody fun too.

Jack started up the dune again, the sand crumbling away with each weary step before he pulled up with a start.

*Laughter.*

The same girlish, flirtatious laughter he thought he'd heard before back in the cottage. It was impossible to tell where it was coming from over the tortured howls of the wind. In fact, it was hard to be sure he'd actually heard anything.

He swept the beam back and forth, the torch powerful enough to cut through the rain and seemingly illuminate the low clouds above the fringe of marram grass atop the dune. There was nothing bar the rain hitting the sodden sand and wet, rustling grass hissing all about him in the darkness.

It must have been his imagination. Again.

How many times could he hear a girl laughing and be imagining it?

Maybe it was a bird nesting in the dunes. The lesser spotted flirt perhaps? A giggle-finch? A tawny twirly-girlybird? Jack knew no more about birds than the next Londoner; pigeons delighted in shitting on your car and on a really good day they managed to shit on you too. Beyond that; nothing much. He supposed it might be possible. Especially distorted by the rain and wind.

But it damn well sounded like a girl.

He pushed on, his grip tightening on the torch, the plastic handles of which were slick with rain.

As he neared the summit of Mount Dune, the clumps of marram grass grew thicker and he had to pick a path through them, the wet stems brushing against his jeans like long, dripping fingers. By the time he crested the top his panted breath was coming out in jagged clouds of steam.

The top of the dune seemed to have been scooped out, like a crater atop a volcano, and, for an instant it seemed a group of figures were clustered in a loose circle at the bottom of the pit. Jack nearly dropped the torch, but when he finally focussed on the scene he realised they were not figures at all, but thick trunks of wood thrusting out of the sand like a copse of dead wizened trees.

Jack didn't know any more about trees than he did birds, but he was pretty sure they didn't grow atop sand dunes, even a massive one like this.

He carefully picked his way down the slope, the beam of his torch cutting back and forth trying to find any sign of Moira. Like a smouldering pair of beaten red baseball boots, for instance.

By the time he reached the wooden circle, he'd seen nothing to suggest Moira had been here. Or anyone else. It looked like the perfect secluded spot for the local kids to come and mess about, drink, get high and to, what his parents had euphemistically referred to as, "court," but there was no sign it had been visited recently. Perhaps it was too remote and too much of a slog to get to. Kids today...

Up close he could see the wooden pillars were driftwood someone had seen fit to haul up here and insert into the sand like fence posts. Seven in total. Cracked, knotted and weather-smoothed each one stood taller than Jack.

He placed a hand upon the nearest and gave it a light shove, expecting it to move, but it didn't budge. How big must they be to have enough buried under the sand to be so solidly inserted? Very big, was his rough guesstimated calculation.

And why bother?

He shrugged and moved slowly around the circle. There was no accounting for the strangeness of people. Particularly the ones who lived out in these godforsaken spots away from

28

civilised folk and all the amenities of modern life.

They looked like they'd been here a long time, but he was sure they couldn't be that old. He'd heard of stone circles of course, like Stonehenge, that were thousands of years old, but wood would have long since rotted away and the dunes would not be stable enough anyway, he was sure they moved over time with the wind and winter storms. Still, something about the knotted, twisted wood, worn smooth by the sand and salt coarsened wind, sang an old, old song.

He circled the slopes of Mount Dune's "crater" looking for signs of Moira. If she'd been here, the rain had smoothed away any sign of her footprints, only his own tracks puncturing the sand were visible.

If she'd been speared by lightning, it hadn't happened here and he couldn't spend the night wandering The Burrows. His jeans were already soaked to his skin and he'd begun to shiver now he was no longer labouring up the slopes of the dune field.

He could come back in the morning if she didn't reappear, though by then he'd really have to think about calling the police.

He'd reached the far lip of the crater and stared out across the dunes, which stretched away along the beach in rolling folds until disappearing into the darkness beyond the reach of his torch.

At what point did he call the police?

He looked up at the weeping sky and let the rain trickle down his face. If she didn't reappear he would have to, wouldn't he? And how would he answer their questions and where would they lead them? Would it make the papers?

Stories about pretty girls always seemed more likely to. And even if they didn't and he went home alone, how long before the police came to his door to ask more questions? If a body turned up, they surely would. Especially if it hadn't been lightning.

People being murdered by strangers was rare. It was usually someone they knew. A family member, friend… a lover. Yes, they'd be questions for sure.

*When was the last time you saw her alive, Mr Orford? What was your relationship with Miss Saunders, exactly? Just why did she run off? Had you argued? Had you scared her?*

Then Amanda would know. Everybody would know. His marriage would be over. He could kiss goodbye to being made partner too, even if that was something he'd gradually stopped working for years ago anyway.

*Shit…*

He rubbed the rain out of his eyes with the palm of his hand and flicked the water away.

Could somebody have grabbed her? He hadn't seen anyone else, but dunes were a good place to hide. Sadly, judging by what he saw in the newspapers, plenty of men would hurt a good-looking young woman given half a chance. In the city, you took precautions. You saw the girl home, you kept an eye out for people watching too keenly, people with drug-addled features or mad staring eyes. But out here, with the yokels…

Years ago he'd taken Amanda to see *Deliverance* at the cinema. She'd joked afterwards how Jack looked a bit like Burt Reynolds, just without the sex appeal. Ha, bloody ha. She hadn't been much taken with the film, but it had stuck with him. Hillbillies doing despicable things to stray city folk...

He tried to shake the thought away. Ok, maybe this was remote by British standards, and the yokels might drink cider and be overly fond of their livestock, but... *really?*

He started to circle the rim of Mount Dune. He was spooking himself, he knew. What if the voice he'd heard in the dunes earlier hadn't been Moira? What if it had been some madman she'd stumbled across? Jack couldn't help but wonder if some slobbering, slack-jawed inbred was watching him blunder about The Burrows, a powerful show-off torch advertising his presence. Someone who was sniggering wetly into his hand and whispering to his cousin, who was probably also his father, about what fun they were going to have with this particular little piggy...

He was halfway around the rim, wading through waist-high clumps of marram grass when he froze, jerking the torch beam back to something it had illuminated down in the crater. Not a hillbilly, but something that made his heart race and mouth dry just the same.

He scrambled down towards the circle of twisted, weathered wooden columns and grabbed something snagged in the centre of a clump of grass.

A jacket.

It was crumpled and damp with rain, but he recognised the cracked abused leather well enough.

Moira's jacket.

*Shit. Shit. Shit!!!*

He turned it over. Other than being soaked it appeared undamaged; there were no rips or tears. No blood either, as

31

far as he could see.

Heart pounding and eyes wide he flicked the torch beam across all the nearby clumps of grass, but there was no other sign of Moira.

He drew in a big shuddering breath, the wet air tasted faintly of salt and sand.

Maybe a lightning strike could blow your clothes off (had he heard that somewhere?) but it didn't seem likely. And if it had, Moira's body wouldn't be far away. The jacket was too weighty to have been dragged anywhere much, even in this wind.

So why the hell else would she have taken her jacket off in this foul weather? She wouldn't have of course. But a rapist or murderer might well have ripped it from her as he... as he...

Jack staggered into the driftwood circle and leaned against one of the wet, smooth columns for support. His legs suddenly felt like they were about to give way and it had nothing to do with the unaccustomed exercise they'd had to endure. He wanted to vomit. His breath echoed wetly in his ears and he pulled back his hood, hoping the cutting rain might shock some sense back into his stuttering mind.

He had to get help now. For the first time the rational part of him, as opposed to his overactive imagination that had been spooked and inflated by the eerie compressing darkness swirling about him, accepted something awful must have befallen Moira. Nothing else made sense.

He would have to get back to the cottage and phone the police. He could imagine some local copper eventually rolling up at the House of Shells, pissed off at being dragged out here in the middle of the night. Probably ruddy-faced and eyes full of scorn as Jack described Moira and what had happened.

*"And what is your relationship with this young woman exactly Mr Orford? Twenty-three you said, wasn't it? I see Sir. Twenty. Three. Years. Old. Not your daughter, I take it?"*

What else could he do? He couldn't just run off back to London and leave her. She might not be dead. She might be still out here on The Burrows, beaten, bloody and probably raped. But still alive.

Jack's fingers gripped the rain-slicked jacket.

He could just go. Nothing was linking him to this place. Moira had made the arrangements, he could just go back to London and nobody would know. They'd be no questions, no blank, uncomprehending look on Amanda's face slowly melting into hurt and rage. His life would go back to normal...

He shook his head. The rain was trickling down his face in cold meandering streams. Get back to the house. One thing at a time. That was best, wasn't it? He wasn't going to run. He wasn't that much of an arsehole. Was he? No, of course not. He was a good guy. He'd do the right thing in the end. He'd get help. But, for now, one thing at a time. Get back to the cottage.

He straightened up, the torch played across the centre of the wooden circle; it was about twenty feet across. He hadn't noticed before, but the sand between the driftwood trunks was completely smooth. It was like someone had taken a trowel to it and flattened away every last imperfection. No grass grew, no ripples crumpled the sand. No little scraps of wood or dead grass stems. Nothing.

Something was odd about the driftwood pillars too. No graffiti. Nothing carved into them, no teenage penknives had hacked misspelt words of undying love into the old soft wood, no initials inside crudely chipped hearts.

Well, it wasn't London, was it? The kids around here probably had better things to do. Like rape and murder maybe.

Jack swept the torch about him again, playing it along the rim of Mount Dune, trying to spear any knife-wielding, slack-jawed yokels sneaking up on him in its beam. Still nothing.

It didn't seem entirely likely. If Moira had befallen some lunatic, why would they linger around the crime scene?

The marram grass was swishing about him, the wind picking up again, a sibilant hiss, primal and mocking.

What the fuck do you know, little piggy?

Jack sucked in air, he could see his tracks on the far side of the circle, he just needed to follow them to get back down to the boardwalk and the House of Shells. And doors with locks on. And a telephone.

And the car.

Still gripping Moira's jacket, he ran through the centre of the wooden circle. The ground was flat enough here not to have to worry about stumbling.

At least until the torch died with a faint popping sound.

Jack staggered to a halt with a cry as a wave of darkness rushed in to engulf him.

"You must be fucking joking!"

He shook the torch in disgust, finding the switch and clicking it back and forth until he accepted it was dead. That little popping noise. The bulb must have blown. Amanda and her shitty presents...

The blackness was almost total, without the torch he could see nothing. For one awful moment, he considered the possibility the torch was working fine and he'd just gone blind.

Stupid. His night sight hadn't adjusted thanks to the power of the torch beam. Not enough for such a black, moonloos, starless night anyway

He couldn't blunder on through The Burrows in total darkness. He only had to keep going in the same direction to make his way back to the boardwalk, but blind he'd stumble over some dip or marram grass clump and probably turn his ankle. Or worse. The sand was soft, but if he went head over tit hard enough he could still do himself a serious injury. Break his neck even.

He'd have to wait, let his eyes adjust. How long would that take? Ten minutes? Twenty?

He stood motionless, listening to the rain patter on the drenched sand and willing his eyes to find forms in the utter black surrounding him.

Then he remembered the torch had two lights. There was also the orange hazard light on top, the one that could be set to flash if your car broke down on some dark road. Not so good for illuminating, but enough for him to pick out his footprints in the sand and follow them out of The Burrows. He dropped Moira's jacket and fiddled with the torch, finding the second switch and clicking it over. Nothing happened.

That would just be too fucking easy, wouldn't it?

He was still facing the right way, he hadn't moved since

the torch gave out, so he could, at least, feel his way across the centre of the wooden circle where it was flat, till he found one of the driftwood pillars on the far side. Only a few paces but anything that got him closer to being out of The Burrows worked for him.

He'd half stooped to find Moira's jacket when the laughter came again. Clearer. Closer. And somehow more... urgent?

A giggle-finch?

He stayed in a half crouch, feeling his feet sinking a little into the saturated sand. That really didn't sound like any bird, did it? And, anyway, birds didn't sing at night. That's why you had a dawn chorus as they chirped and tweeted their welcome to the sun. At night, like all sensible creatures, they were tucked up in their nests, probably watching the *Two Ronnies* on TV or trying to make little birds. The only animals out and about at night were the predators. The ones looking for supper. Something soft and tasty; like a lost little piggy.

"Moira?"

His voice sounded small and feeble; instantly swallowed by the swirling rain-washed night.

Something brushed against his boot.

He cried out and jumped backwards. Peering down into the darkness around his feet. What the hell had that been? He hadn't imagined it; something had brushed against the side of his boot. A mouse maybe? A rat?

Jack's heart was thumping. He'd never been scared of the dark, even as a kid. Just because you couldn't see every dark nook and cranny, it didn't mean anything dangerous was lurking.

Now, however, he was bloody terrified of it.

Was there another sound? Above the rhythm of the falling rain? The faint plop and sigh of sand slowly being disturbed?

The giggle-finch gave another titter, directly ahead of him. This time, it sounded almost hysterical.

Then something pressed against the toes of his boot. Something that felt like, but, of course, couldn't possibly be, grasping fingers...

# Four

Jack gave a strangled cry, jerked his foot away and then ran. Something snagged the flare of his jeans making him stagger before he managed to yank it free and regain his balance.

It was terrifying running hell for leather in complete darkness, but not half so terrifying as standing still.

Sounds were coming out of the night all around him; scraping, rasping, scratching, wet, squelching plops. Not loud, but loud enough.

Jack screamed as something hit his right shoulder, hard enough to send him spinning to the ground and skidding through the wet sand on his knees. The torch slipped from his hands and he heard it thudding on the sand. The impact must have jarred something in the wiring, as the orange hazard light that had refused to work before, stuttered into life and began blinking on and off.

It was designed to warn, not illuminate, but its intermittent light was enough for Jack to see the blow he'd taken on the shoulder had not been from an assailant, but one of the twisted driftwood pillars he'd blindly managed to run into. A foot to the right and he'd have charged head first into it, probably knocking himself unconscious in the process.

Still clutching Moira's jacket, Jack scrambled to his feet and retrieved the torch, immeasurably grateful for the pulsing orange light the hazard was throwing out.

Until he looked behind him anyway.

The sand, which had been so perfectly smooth before, was now rippling, buckling and erupting as if Mount Dune really was a volcano with lava bubbling to the surface of its caldera.

The scene was like some jerky stop-motion student art film, blinking between complete darkness and a pale orange glow. It illuminated the night only just sufficiently to show something pulling itself out of the sand. Or rather some *things*, for multiple dark shadows were heaving themselves from the clinging wet sand and into the cutting rain.

There was laughter too. Not the girlish, playful laughter of the giggle-finch, but howls of dry, cackling, gibbering glee.

The nearest, and best lit, shape consisted of two spindly arms leveraging up a sand-encrusted head and shoulders. He could make out no features in the weak light, just sand falling away in the rain as more of the torso emerged from the dune.

Then he was running. Thrusting the torch out ahead of him but taking no care to pick a path through the marram grass, he simply sprinted through it and up the slope to the rim of the dune. He could hear nothing but screams and it wasn't until he crested the ridge that he realised they were his.

Jack hurdled over the rim and tried to sprint down the slope. His legs lost purchase almost immediately, his arms fly wheeling to keep balance, but momentum took him over and he was rolling down the slope, grass tearing at him as he tumbled past. His mouth and eyes alternatively filled with sand and rain until he came to a thudding halt at the bottom of the dune.

Dazed and panting, he lay prone on the sand staring up at a sky alternating between black and orange.

*I didn't see that. I just didn't.*

His fingers clawed at the sand, the sodden grains pushing under his nails and filling the pores of his skin. The rain was dripping down his face and seeping up through the seat of his jeans.

*Can't just lay here. Relaxing as it is. Might catch my death...*

Jack sat up and spat out the portion of the dune he'd tried to eat during his rolling tumble.

The torch was three or four yards behind and above him. Blinking patiently, just doing its job and advising of a hazard ahead.

His eyes were pulled up the slope of Mount Dune, past the circle of orange light and the rain slashing through it. He couldn't see the top of the dune, the hazard warning just wasn't casting enough light; it was a black, wet nothingness. But between the patter of the rain, the hiss of the grass and the constant rumble of the distant surf he could hear maniacal laughter and beneath that something else, a clicking, chattering noise Jack couldn't confidently identify.

However, it did sound an awful lot like teeth clicking together.

*Here little piggy, we're sooo hungry...*

What had he seen? Precisely? It had looked like figures –

he couldn't say people – pulling themselves out the sand. But that was nonsense.

The laughter was getting louder. Whatever he *had* seen, it was coming down the slope of the big dune. Towards him.

*After him.*

He clambered to his feet. He'd been lucky. Nothing seemed broken or sprained. He considered leaving the torch, he didn't like the idea of carrying a big flashing light to show exactly where he was, but the thought of ploughing through the dunes in complete darkness was worse.

It meant moving back towards them, even if it was only a couple of paces up the slope. All he wanted to do was put as much distance between himself and whatever was rollicking down the dune, whooping and a hollering by the sound of it.

He scrambled forward and grabbed the torch, never taking his eyes off the flickers of orange light it cast up the slope. There was no sign of Moira's jacket.

He still couldn't see anything. But that damn shrieking *was* getting closer.

Jack turned and ran down the slope though at a less hectic pace. He didn't fancy somersaulting down another dune. He might not be so lucky if he tried that stunt again.

The surf was to his right, an entirely sane and normal sound, so he was sure he was heading in the right direction. The dune slopes were kinder back to the boardwalk and he was more worried about tripping over a clump of marram grass. His side was starting to ache and he had to stop for a second to spit coppery saliva. Most of it landed on his chin. He didn't even have enough breath left to spit properly.

He looked back over his shoulder. The screeching had

faded to the point he wasn't even sure he could hear it, but he pushed on with more of a stagger than a run. The wet sand seemed to be sucking at his feet, making every stride an ordeal.

He'd only taken a few steps when he heard the girlish giggling come again, this time to his left beyond the reach of the flashing hazard light. The sound was entirely different to the things behind him, but he was pretty sure it wasn't Moira either. He blundered on a little further, only to be confronted by a sandbank thick with marram grass rising above his head. He could probably clamber over it eventually, but he was sure he hadn't come through it on the way up the dune.

The giggle-finch sounded again off to his left, the tone seemed different. More insistent. Calling him? Shit, his imagination was in overdrive. He looked wildly about, he still couldn't see anything but the grass and the rain, but beyond the gusting howls of wind, the sound of mad chattering glee was rolling down the dune again. Getting closer.

He turned left and stumbled along the bank of grass in the direction he'd heard the giggle-finch. After no more than a dozen paces the orange blinking light showed the ridge of marram grass dropping away and the slope stretching on down uninterrupted into the darkness.

By the time he finally staggered onto the boardwalk, he was gasping for breath and sweat was mixing with the sand and rain on his face. A faint glow tinged the sky towards the end of the boardwalk. He'd left the lights on back at the cottage. Thankfully.

The marram grass was thrashing around the boardwalk.

Tinged orange by the flashing hazard light they looked nightmarish and alien. Though nothing was going to beat what he'd seen on the top of that fucking dune in the nightmare stakes.

Jack looked at the blinking orange light in his hands, before, in a moment that he wasn't sure was inspiration or desperation, he hurled it as far as he could into the dunes on the other side of the boardwalk.

If he was being chased maybe they'd carry on after the hazard rather than follow him back all the way to the house. He didn't have a lot to work with, but he was hoping they weren't the brightest monsters in town. He didn't want to think what those things were and even less what they wanted with him, but he wasn't hanging around to find out. He only needed a couple of minutes to get back to the car. And once he got out of here he wasn't stopping till he got back to the streetlights, pollution and sanity of London.

# Five

A car was something that got you from A to B. Period. Jack had never understood the guys who spent hours eulogising and comparing different makes and models, the kind who were never entirely happy unless their head was buried in the guts of an engine and their clothes were suitably grimed with grease and oil.

But when Jack staggered off the boardwalk and stumbled around the bending path leading to the House of Shells, he didn't think he'd ever seen anything so beautiful as his dark blue Ford Cortina Mark IV 2.0L Ghia sitting patiently for him in the yellowish light spilling from the cottage.

He would, he solemnly swore, never ever roll his eyes when his cousin Kev started off about sump oil or spark plugs again.

Jack slumped against the car, resting his palms on the cold, wet, metallic reassurance of the roof to confirm it really was there. And to touch something that didn't feel of sand.

How long had he been out on The Burrows? Probably no more than an hour, ninety minutes at most, but he felt like he'd been there for days. Despite the constant rain, his throat was dry and gritty from the mouthfuls of sand he'd taken tumbling down Mount Dune. His head and side ached like he'd done a few rounds with Rocky.

*What about Moira?*

She'd been atop that dune where those things had erupted from the sand. Her jacket proved it. And she hadn't come back. He could do the math.

Whatever he'd seen up there, whatever he'd damn well felt grabbing at his feet, he couldn't do anything for her now. He wasn't staying here. He'd go back to London, if the police came, so be it.

But what would he tell them?

That monstrous gibbering things lived in a big dune by the sea and they'd gobbled Moira up? The only dilemma for the police would be whether to send him to prison or the funny farm.

*What if Moira hadn't told anyone where she was going?*

Maybe she didn't want her friends to know she was seeing an older married man (particularly one that looked a bit like Burt Reynolds, but without the sex appeal). He'd never even seen any of her friends. She wouldn't take him back to her bedsit, "It's too small and I make too much noise," she'd explained with a grin. Even when he'd picked her up that morning she'd been waiting outside, sitting on the wall rather than getting him to knock and come in. Actually, he didn't even know which house she lived in; she'd only given him the street.

The only thing linking him to Moira was his bag, sitting in the hallway. She'd arranged the cottage, everything else was hers.

Jack glanced down the path to The Burrows. His heart still hammering and his feet still itching to get away from this place before something monstrous came bowling out of the night. The rain was easing off, but the clouds hadn't broken and little could be seen beyond the pool of light thrown out by the House of Shells.

With a shaking hand, Jack unlocked the car, at the third attempt, and climbed into the comforting cocooning smell of velour and vinyl mixed with the barest hint of petrol fumes.

It wasn't cowardice. There was nothing he could do for Moira and no one he could turn to for help. No one would believe him. He wasn't even sure if he believed him.

A few minutes and he'd be on the road, heading back to civilisation.

He thought of his bag sitting in the hallway; clothes, toiletries and a couple of paperbacks. Nothing to identify him.

*Shit.*

Sitting at the bottom of his bag was a folder of building specs he'd thought he might have a chance to flick through if Moira gave him a spare five minutes. He wasn't even sure why he'd brought them. There was no great rush on that job.

He supposed he'd just wanted to impress Moira. Look at me with my big important work to do. Don't you worry your pretty head, this is Very Important Stuff that absolutely Must Be Done, but it won't take long, promise.

*Idiot.*

The drawings and papers had the firm name on them. Might as well have his bloody home address plastered over them.

He stared at The Burrows through the beads of rainwater clinging to the windscreen; he thought he could make out the faint orange blink of the hazard light though he couldn't be sure. He wasn't as prepared to believe his eyes as much as he had up to an hour or so ago.

If something was coming after him, wouldn't they have got here by now?

Jack slipped the key into the ignition.

He was certain the engine wasn't going to turn. The battery was flat, sand had gotten somewhere vital or the spark plugs were blown. You should regularly check your spark plugs; cousin Kev was always telling him that. The boring git.

Instead, the engine sprang to life with a healthy growl and Jack let out a breath he hadn't been aware he'd been holding.

He hit the headlights and filled the damp air with piercing, blessed light. The beams cut through the darkness, illuminating nothing but falling jewels of rain and the track that carried on parallel to The Burrows.

The Cortina would need to be turned, he didn't know if the lane re-joined a road further on and he was in no mood to find out. There was a small grass verge by the side of the cottage, just enough for him to reverse the car in and out of a three-point turn. He eased the Cortina back till it was facing the direction of The Burrows and the headlights picked out the path down to the boardwalk. Flicking the headlights to full beam, he was able to make out the first dunes beyond the trees.

Nothing moved bar the rain.

*Two minutes. Two minutes to grab my bag and then it'll be like I was never here. And I can forget whatever it was I saw up there.*

*Or thought I saw...*

He listened to the idling engine and then, reluctantly, pushed open the door and hobbled through the front garden. His side was really hurting now. Could he have cracked a rib?

He found the front door key and pushed inside. The dull yellow light greeted him. It had looked so bright when he'd been outside, but now it seemed gloomy and oppressive.

His bag was where he'd left it. He ignored both Moira's duffel and the hot stab of guilt twisting through him to snatch it up. Then he remembered the clothes he'd kicked off in the kitchen.

Men's clothes would raise more questions. Jack hurried through and grabbed the first load of soaked clothes he'd worn earlier. He slung them over the bag. A bottle of water poked out of the grocery bag. He grabbed that too and was done.

He noticed a trail of sand through the house where he'd just walked. Glancing down he was unsurprised to see wet sand caked his jeans and coat.

He might be running away from The Burrows, but he'd be taking a hell of a lot of it home with him.

He hurried back to peer around the front door, the headlights were still showing nothing but the rain, finally slowing to a fine drizzle. He gave one final look over his shoulder to ensure he hadn't forgotten anything.

Clumps of wet sand smattered the stairs.

They must have fallen off him earlier. Except... he'd changed out of his wet clothes before going upstairs. The sand would have dried to powder by now anyway.

"Moira?"

He called, in a half hesitant, half hopeful voice.

What if she'd gotten back to the cottage while he'd been bouncing around the dunes? She might be upstairs, asleep and blissfully unaware of the... *things* out in The Burrows. He took a single step back into the house.

What if it was one of those *things?*

*"Moira!"*

This time, he shouted.

He looked over his shoulder, through the open door the headlights still showed nothing. He ventured as far as the foot of the stairs. Clumps of sand were scattered on each step, some a little to the left, some a little to the right. Now he was closer he could see beads of water splashed here and there too. Someone had dripped rainwater as well as sand as they'd climbed the stairs. And not very long ago either.

The front and back doors had been shut and he hadn't noticed any broken windows, whoever it was had to have a key to get in. So it must be Moira! He placed a foot on the first step.

Or someone who had Moira's key.

Or *something...*

Jack thought of those dark, sand-encrusted forms hauling themselves out of the dune and their maniacal, howling laughter. If they'd killed Moira they would have her key. But would they know how to use it?

Was he prepared to bet his life on it?

A creak came from upstairs.

Footsteps on floorboards?

"Moira..."

Or just the frame of the cottage settling and shifting in the damp air?

No answer came. If Moira was here she would have answered him. So either no one was upstairs or something was up there. Either way, he didn't need to go up those steep, narrow stairs looking for whatever had dropped sand onto each step.

He shuffled away, not wanting to turn his back to either the stairs or the front door. He was halfway across the living room when someone giggled.

His heart jumped halfway up his throat and he looked wildly around. The room was empty. He wasn't sure quite where the giggle had come from, it sounded like it could have been either upstairs or in the living room.

He fought the urge to sprint back out into the night and the monsters living in it.

"Moira? Is that you?"

The giggle came again. This time it sounded much closer. And he was sure it wasn't Moira. Her giggle was deeper and, somehow, *dirtier*, occasionally collapsing into a snorting noise that should have been charmless but had always made him laugh along with her regardless. No, this was entirely different. Lighter, lilting and playful. The same as he'd heard out on The Burrows earlier.

The Giggle-finch.

The laughter came again, so close it felt it had been in his ear and he spun around expecting to see... something? But the room was still empty and he heard nothing above his thumping heart bar the soft patter of rain outside.

He edged towards the door.

The giggle didn't sound threatening. More playful. Maybe even come-hither. And the Giggle-finch *had* helped him on The Burrows, leading him back down the dunes when that ridge of marram grass had blocked his path.

But still.

There was nobody in the room.

"Is anybody here?"

The cottage was silent and he knew he was wasting time. He should either check upstairs or get going, but he was convinced now somebody else was here. He could feel no ghostly presence, no cold malign spirit, the hairs on the back of his neck were damp with sweat and rain but they definitely weren't standing up. But, all the same, he knew he wasn't alone in the House of Shells

"Who are you?"

This time he did hear something; a dripping noise he'd probably heard before but hadn't been able to distinguish from the rain outside. In front of the TV a small puddle of water had formed, the kind that might collect beneath someone who'd just hurried in out of the rain. As he stared a drop of water plopped into the little puddle, sending concentric rings shimmering across its surface. Jack glanced up at the ceiling expecting – and hoping – to see a leak, but there was nothing.

*Plop.*

Another drip. Had it just appeared in mid-air?

Jack took a small step forward. He was planning to put his hand over the puddle to see where the drips of water were falling from when his eye caught his reflection in the dead screen of the TV. He could see both himself and the room distorted in the curved glass.

And something else.

Another figure, standing where that puddle was; blurry and indistinct. It looked for all the world like a slightly framed girl wrapped in sodden rags, dark hair falling past her shoulders in twisted rat's tails. He could only see her from behind, but he knew she was staring at him. Her hands hung loosely at her sides and water dripping from her fingertips.

The figure in the black mirror of the TV giggled, her narrow shoulders twitching up and down as she did.

That was enough for Jack.

He scrambled out of the cottage and slammed the door shut after him. One eye on The Burrows he threw his things onto the passenger seat, then popped the boot. After a few seconds, his fingers closed around the cold steel of a tyre iron. He'd never hit anything with a tyre iron before, he'd never even changed a tyre with one for that matter, but it felt hefty and solid enough in his hand.

Still gripping the tyre iron, Jack slammed the boot shut and then leant into the car. If Moira was upstairs, there was a better way of waking her up than going back inside with whatever else was in the House of Shells.

The horn was loud enough in the still quiet night to make Jack jump and he'd been expecting it. Eyes on the lit upstairs window that he could see obliquely from where he'd backed the car, he kept hitting the horn, till it sounded like the furious bellows of some stranded beast plaintively crying in distress.

No face appeared at the window, no sleepy shout or dozy

protest about the noise.

Nothing.

Then, in the distance, came hoots and cries; harsh, rasping and hysterical. The howls of jabbering lunatics to Jack's ears. Jabbering lunatics mimicking the sound of a car horn anyway.

"Moira! If you're there, come out. *Now!!!*" He screamed. So loudly he thought his throat might rip.

No reply came from the house, though something howled like a loon out on the darkened Burrows and that was enough.

He slammed the car door shut and hit the lock, then made sure all the others were locked. He sat panting for a second then started to turn the car down the track towards the road and the sane world. Moira wasn't in the cottage. And whatever the Giggle-finch was, if it was anything at all, he didn't want to see it any more than the things that had burst from the sand atop Mount Dune.

As the headlights swung round they illuminated figures, three or four at least, hobbling out of The Burrows. It was only a second before they scurried, shrieking away from the light, but it was enough for Jack to make out forms that were tall, thin, angular and encased in sand. Long tattered hair hanging lankly past thin bony shoulders. They were all naked other than for wet clinging sand and they all appeared, after a fashion, to be female. But more than that, the image that stuck with Jack was of their mouths, which were all hanging open, far too open, huge black maws that gaped to the size of a fully spread hand.

The track was no more than a rutted, potted dirt and sand

gap between the trees, and now it was sodden and sprinkled with sizeable puddles. At night, even in good conditions, it was best traversed at little more than walking pace in a car.

Jack put his foot down and sped off fast enough for the darkened trees and bushes to blur past him.

The car rolled and bumped with every divot, rut and pothole it ploughed through, but Jack kept his foot down and his eyes on the narrow gap between the wooded slope on the left and the sparser, smaller trees on the right separating the little road from the first dunes of The Burrows. What he didn't do was glance at the rear-view mirror.

He never wanted to see what was behind him again.

It took an especially bone-jarring jolt that left the taste of blood in his mouth to make him pull his foot from the accelerator. He'd put enough distance between himself and the House of Shells now, and even if more of those things were ahead of him, he'd just drive straight through them. He wasn't stopping till he got back to London.

Once he'd slowed to a saner pace he fumbled for the bottle of water he'd collected from the cottage and downed half of it in greedy slurps, though as much went down his front as his mouth thanks to the roll and bump of the car. His throat felt raw. Sand, shouting and being scared shitless could do that, he guessed.

He tried to force the image of those creatures from his head, but the only thing he could replace them with was the certainty that he'd left Moira to them.

What if she'd somehow managed to get away from them had staggered around The Burrows injured before finally making it back to the house?

She could have collapsed upstairs. Not asleep, but unconscious. He could have hired a brass band to march up and down and it still wouldn't have roused her. Why hadn't he just gone upstairs to make sure?

Had he left her to those nightmarish creatures because of something he thought he'd seen reflected in a TV screen?

And what the fuck were they anyway!?

Something a damn sight worse than hillbillies, that was for sure. Words kept popping into his head. Stupid, preposterous names that would buy him a one-way ticket to some pretty heavy sedation.

Ghosts? Ghouls? Zombies? Aliens?

Medical students?

It would have been a ridiculous prank to bury yourself in the sand and wait for some fool to wander by to scare shitless. Even if Moira had been in on it, who was going to hide all night in the sand to trick anyone, let alone a stranger. No, it was ludicrous.

More ludicrous than... Ghosts? Ghouls? Zombies? Aliens?

He hoped it was just a trick, even if it had half frightened him to death. If it wasn't, then the world was a far darker and more terrifying place than he'd ever imagined.

Jack peered over the steering wheel, leaning forward. It had taken a good few minutes to drive down to the House of Shells from the turn-off, but he'd been driving the whole way like a sane, responsible motorist rather than Evil Knievel on a promise. The exit should be coming up soon and he didn't want a drunk farmer coming home from the pub on his tractor to succeed where the Burrows-Things had failed.

On the assumption they hadn't just wanted to ask him for

a cup of milk.

He giggled.

He sounded almost as mad as they did.

Fuck it. A little bit longer and he'd be on a tarmacked road again, albeit a hedge lined yokel back road only wide enough for one car, but it would take him to a proper road eventually, and that would take him all the way home. He'd find a late-night radio station and sing every damn song at the top of his voice as he drove.

Just so long as there was nothing by *The Clash.*

Jack frowned, a small building was coming up on his left. He'd been sure the House of Shells had been the first and only dwelling they'd seen trundling down the track when they'd arrived. He supposed he must have missed it, perhaps it was right by the turn-off and he'd been too busy trying to not totally screw the Cortina's suspension to notice it.

Somebody was still up as the lights were on. Should he warn them? There were these things that had erupted from the top of The Burrows. Ugly things with big gaping mouths and wearing nothing but sand. Monsters was a good word for them. He wasn't entirely sure, but he thought they were probably both insane and dangerous. Yes, that –

His frown deepened, people were up ahead, milling about on either side of the narrow track. Some kind of party, though it really wasn't the right weather for a barbeque or al fresco drinking. He slowed the car to a crawl; running down a drunken teenager would just about cap his night.

One of the figures lurched into the track, then span sharply away as the car's headlights caught them.

Jack found his mouth was hanging open. Not so much

because the figure was too tall, thin, angular and encrusted with sand. Or that its mouth was a gaping chasm as it snarled, covered its eyes and scurried into the shadows of the verge.

But because the cottage with its lights on was the House of Shells...

# Six

Jack's mind had never *actually* reeled before.

Even when the Burrows-Things had erupted from the ground, grabbing at his ankles, or when he'd lain stunned at the bottom of Mount Dune with a gob full of sand listening to their mad, snickering howls. He'd still, more or less, been in control.

It was like cycling down a steep hill at full pelt, the wheels were spinning too furiously for the chain to catch and if you tried to hit the brakes you'd either go into a mad, uncontrollable skid or you'd tumble arse and tit over the handlebars. All you could do was go with it and wait for the speed to burn off when the hill flattened out.

However, this time, he wasn't sure the hill was ever going to flatten out.

His mind was spinning furiously, but the chain wasn't catching on any damn thing.

Being chased by a bunch of ugly-arsed monsters was one thing. Mad maybe, but Jack was prepared to admit there could be plenty of shit in the world he, and maybe the rest of humanity, knew nothing about. More things in Heaven and Earth etc. But he'd just driven down a road. A straight fucking road! You can't drive down a straight road and come back to the same place. The world didn't work like that. Not the normal sane world of cars and coffee and football and beer and beautiful young women who might seduce you for no obvious reason. And even in the other world. The world of gibbering, howling *things*. Even their fucking world shouldn't work like that!

*It was a straight road. A straight road! A straight as an arrow going nowhere but one place fucking road!*

There must have been another turning, one he'd missed before and as he'd hell for leathered it away from the House of Shells he'd taken it and it had looped round, re-joined the original track further along the shore and brought him back to the House of Shells. Had to be.

*Except...*

Hills rose steeply to the left of the track. Any side turn would have to go up the hill and then down again to bring him back. And he hadn't gone up or down any hills! He was sure he would have noticed. On this bumpy, divot strewn, pitiful backwater excuse for a road even if he hadn't noticed it the Cortina damn well would have!

Jack was gripping the wheel hard enough to turn his knuckles white. He eased off and realised the car had come to a halt, the engine idling. He took a deep breath and shuddered. Closed his eyes and opened them again.

*Ok, we do this again and do it slowly.*

He re-checked the doors, back and front. They were all locked. Nothing was getting into the car. He was safe.

He focused on the road ahead and the House of Shells. The Burrows-Things had scattered and scurried into the shadows. They didn't seem at all keen on the Cortina's headlights, which were still on full beam. Good. He really wasn't too keen on them either.

They could lurk in the trees and bushes and gibber to their heart's content. He would just roll by and this time he would pay attention. A straight road. It was a *straight* road and it was going to take him back to the straight world of street lights, and road signs and cheesy late-night radio and crap motorway services with overpriced barely edible sandwiches. *Para-fucking-dise* in other words.

He eased his foot on the accelerator and nudged the car forwards. He could see the Burrows-Things in the shadows watching him. Hungry and sneaky he thought. But they really didn't like the light. When the edge of the beam caught one, it flinched and jumped away as if burnt, scurrying back into the dark trees.

The Cortina rolled past the House of Shells at a pace that didn't endanger either the car or Jack's bones. And it *was* the House of Shells. Any lingering doubt that it might just look like the cottage were dismissed as the sweep of the headlights caught the sign by the door spelling out its name in cockle shells. The front door, Jack noticed, was shut so they hadn't ventured inside. If Moira was in there...

Beneath his fear and confusion, Jack felt a strange kind of shitty for leaving Moira behind. However, there was no way he was getting out of the car. If he knew she was inside, maybe... but he didn't. And if he got out of the car those things would rip him to shreds. He wasn't a hero, but he wasn't an idiot either.

This time, Jack kept an eye on the rearview mirror once he'd passed the cottage. Burrows-Things scuttled back on to the road, gibbering and waving their thin too-long arms about, a couple followed for a few paces before falling back as the darkness consumed them.

Jack rolled his bottom lip between his teeth and turned his attention fully onto the track ahead. Trees pressed in on both side though sparser on The Burrows side. In daylight, he'd be able to see the dunes through the thinning trees but at night the road, the *straight* road, kept the car's light directly ahead and they didn't cast enough to the sides to pick out anything beyond the trees. If he stopped, turned off the engine and rolled down the window, he'd probably be able to hear the distant rumble of surf, but he really wasn't *that* curious.

He slowed the car further, going at no more than a modest walking pace now. The track was narrow enough for the occasional stray branch to scrape the side of the car. They sounded like dry, bony fingers, and several times Jack jumped and jerked the car forward a little faster.

There was no sign of a turn-off or an alternative track. It was so narrow he really couldn't miss one. There wasn't even room to turn the car, a narrow drainage ditch cut and banked the right-hand side and the trees to the left were hard against the track. Not that he had the slightest desire to turn around.

He tried to remember how long it had taken to drive from the winding little B-road down to the House of Shells, but it was a hazy, fuzzy memory of something that seemed to have happened far longer ago than that afternoon.

He'd never have seen the turning without Moira calling it out. Just a little break in the trees as the B-road turned away to the left and, presumably, cut across the headland he'd seen from atop the dunes.

All he could recall was being tired from the early start and long drive and eager to get into the cottage with Moira. Back in those more innocent times, all he'd been thinking of was getting her into bed and making himself, even more, tired.

It'd been just a few minutes, hadn't it? No more than five, surely. He glanced at the dashboard clock and the milometer; if he'd been paying attention he could have marked the time and distance from the House of Shells. Funny how gibbering monsters could make you miss a trick like that.

He giggled again then stopped himself. Bad habit to get into.

The car trundled on and he resisted the urge to go faster. The Burrows-Things were back at the house and he was determined not to take the same wrong turn he'd taken before. He'd managed to convince himself he *had* taken a wrong turn. There was just no other explanation.

He kept telling himself that as he hunched over the wheel to peer at the grassy ruts of the track as it rolled out of the darkness, right up until the moment he saw the lights of the House of Shells again. Then he swore.

And then he cried.

# Seven

Jack awoke with a dry mouth, a sore neck and a dull ache in his side.

He groaned, peeling open his eyes to squint at the grey watery dawn. The track still stretched out ahead of him. He'd become rather familiar with it during the night. With increasing frustration, he'd driven down it another five times and each journey had, without deviation, returned him to the House of Shells. The only apparent difference being that he hadn't spotted any of the wretched Burrows-Things on his last two drive-bys.

Maybe the joke had worn thin and they'd got bored of laughing at the fool in the Cortina who couldn't find his way off a straight road.

Or they'd just pulled back deeper into the woods to wait for him to get out of the hateful metal box with its bright, nasty lights.

He eyed the verges on either side of him. Thickly wooded slopes to the left, sparser trees and gorse to the right, thinning out to the dunes beyond that he could now make out in the flat morning light. The rain had stopped at some point though the sky was still low and ominous. No Burrows-Things. The way they'd shied and scuttled away from his headlights suggested they were unlikely to be out and about during daylight.

The House of Shells was somewhere behind him. And probably ahead of him too.

Increasingly frustrated and despondent, he'd stopped about half a mile from the cottage. The Cortina's milometer had helpfully informed him it took just over a mile to go to and from the House of Shells. So he was about as far as he could get from the damned place without going back again.

He'd decided to wait for the dawn. Surely, in the reassuring sanity of daylight, he'd be able to find his way off this bloody track? For a while, he'd left the headlights on, but eventually decided he didn't want to drain the battery and had sat and stared into the blackness through the water-jewelled windscreen with just the reading light on. But in the end, he'd killed that too. The thought of the Cortina's battery going flat and being stuck here without light or able to restart the car if the Burrows-Things came calling again, scared him more than the simple darkness.

He hadn't planned to sleep. He didn't think he'd be able to. Possibly ever. But at some point, he'd clearly nodded off and nothing had come tap-tap-tapping at the door in search of a little piggy to wake him up.

He needed a drink, but he'd emptied the water bottle as he'd sat in the darkness. And now nature had taken its inevitable course.

He thought about using the empty bottle, but decided he'd probably end up just peeing all over the car mat.

It was daylight. Safe now. Surely?

Nothing much was moving. A few gulls over The Burrows, some other birds of indeterminate type were chirping out of sight in the trees. But nothing else.

He popped the lock and climbed out of the car, wincing as he found his back was as stiff as his neck.

Jack glanced at the wooded slope. The trees were dark, forebodingly shadowy and clotted with brambles. The other side was far more open and gave a good view of The Burrows, which, he now knew, were home to all kinds of fascinating wildlife not known to the BBC's Natural History department.

He unzipped his still damp jeans and blessed the Cortina's nearside front wheel.

Not a great thank you for saving his life, but, under the circumstances, he was sure his trusty steed would forgive his lack of manners.

After watering the rubber, Jack zipped up, walked to the front of the Cortina and stared down the track which continued as far as he could see until the trees on either side seemed to merge.

"Ok..." he muttered a challenge, "...let's see what this looks like in daylight."

Climbing back in he rubbed away the sleep with the heels of his hands, fired the Cortina up and took her forward, slow and steady. The trees crept by, the jolts were becoming familiar and he passed nothing that either counted as a landmark or out of place.

A little after the milometer dutifully clicked over to a mile from where he'd left the House of Shells for the final time the previous night, he leant over the wheel and slowed to a crawl. A few minutes later the cottage duly reappeared out of the trees on his left.

"Damn it!" Jack slapped the steering wheel hard enough

to sting his palms.

He'd hoped whatever madness had prevented him getting away from this place last night would have passed with the rising sun. But apparently not.

After a moment of staring accusingly at the cottage for stubbornly remaining where it most certainly should not be, Jack climbed back out. He slammed the door behind him, considered locking it, but decided to leave it in case he needed a quick getaway. Or, more likely, a quick getaway and a slow, inevitable return to where he'd started from.

A gull screeched overhead and Jack found himself flinching and whirling round. But it was only a bird, even if it did sound a bit like it was cackling.

The door to the House of Shells was still shut.

He found the key he'd never expected to use again and let himself in. The tyre iron nestled in his right hand. He poked his head around the door but found the front room as he'd left it. He eyed the sand on the floor but was pretty sure there was no more than had dropped off him previously. The sand dusting the stairs was another matter. But again, there was no more than last night, so he dismissed the idea that the Burrow-Things had all headed upstairs for a slumber party while he'd been on his road trip.

First things first.

He headed up the stairs, one step at a time, the tyre iron ready to swing at anything that jumped out. The stairs creaked alarmingly he noticed. That would be quite creepy at night he thought and let out another strangled little giggle.

He followed the trail of sand upstairs, where it petered out on the landing. The door to the bedroom he'd dozed in the previous evening was shut and he could hear nothing. What if Moira had been in there and the Burrows-Things had got in? What if the bedroom was now a charnel house, Moira's blood decorating the walls and her ravaged carcass curled up in the corner? He didn't want to go in. He wanted to run downstairs and drive all the way to London and pretend none of this madness was happening. But he'd tried that and it hadn't worked out too well. Besides, he needed to know.

Jack shouldered open the door and charged into the room in, what he hoped, was a determined, no-nonsense fashion, tyre iron raised above his head.

The bedroom was empty.

Nothing had been disturbed. The room was as it had been when he'd first entered it back in the mists of yesterday.

Jack wandered back onto the landing, tapping the tyre iron against his thigh when he pulled up short and frowned. He went back into the room and stood staring at the bed, or more precisely the pillows and the cream duvet (inevitably embossed with seashells). He'd lain on the bed after his first soaking out on The Burrows, dozing as he'd waited for Moira to return. But the pillows were puffed up and the duvet smooth and unruffled. As if no one had been on the bed the previous night.

Or someone had made the bed.

Of course, no one had broken in to shake up the duvet and puff the pillows up. He was damned sure the House of Shells didn't come with maid service. He must have tidied up the bed himself in expectation of Moira returning. Not that she would have worried about a few crumpled sheets and he certainly wouldn't have, but there was no other explanation.

He'd lain out on the bed and though he hadn't engaged in much restless tossing, the bed should be messed up. Jack shook the thought away and checked the rest of the cottage. He was more interested in looking for monsters.

The back bedroom was unmolested too, free of sand and apparently undisturbed. As was the rest of the house. At least, he hadn't abandoned Moira here then.

Reluctant to put down the tyre iron he stood in the kitchen and swigged water. His stomach protested it wanted something more substantial.

It could wait.

He carried the water back into the front room and slumped on the sofa. It was deep and comfortable. A great sofa for guzzling beer and watching Match of the Day.

His eyes fell on the telephone.

If he couldn't get out, perhaps someone could come and get him. He wasn't entirely sure who he could call or quite how he'd explain himself, but it seemed a decent bet.

*Just say the car broke down and you need a tow. Entirely sane and reasonable.*

And what if they couldn't get out either?

He levered himself off the sofa. That was another bridge, but it was one he soon found he wouldn't have to worry about. The phone was dead. Or almost dead.

He could hear the sea in it.

At first, he thought it was just the blood in his ears, the way you could hear the sea in a shell. But, of course, a dead phone wouldn't do that. It should be silent. And he *could* hear the sea; a constant pounding of big surf hitting the sand like he was standing on a beach. He even heard a gull crying.

Shit, he could even smell it!

Jack slammed the phone down and took a quick step backwards.

Ok, he was in a house by the sea, so not so surprising he could hear the sea and smell it too for that matter.

Except that standing in the middle of the room with the door and windows shut, he couldn't do either.

Jack decided he didn't want to think about it. In fact, he decided he wasn't going to think about anything apart from his stomach, which was starting to kick up a righteous fuss.

They'd bought bacon, bread and butter among other things and Jack was relieved to find the cooker worked perfectly. They'd forgotten to get any ketchup, but under the circumstances that wasn't the worst thing to befall him in the House of Shells. He found an old bottle of vegetable oil in a cupboard and the kitchen was soon filled with the sane and homely aroma of frying bacon, which, Jack realised, was a smell that could make anything seem better.

He polished off two rounds of sandwiches standing by the counter looking out into the back garden, which was wild with rose, jasmine and honeysuckle bushes withering back with the colder autumn nights, and enclosed by a small wall segregating the garden from the dark enclosing woods beyond.

He licked the grease off his fingers when he was done and tossed the pan into the sink before returning to the front room.

He glanced out of the window to make sure none of the local tykes had stolen his car, before trying the TV. It was still too early for the BBC or ITV to be broadcasting, but he couldn't find their test cards as he clicked the dial around. Just static and the hiss of white noise.

Flicking the set off with a grunt of disgust he remained crouched in front of it, staring at his reflection. What had he seen in that dark glass last night? Amongst the other strangeness, it was almost homely. In fact, had he seen anything at all? Probably not. It was just a strung-out imagination and a mind that had seen too many inexplicable things in one night, conjuring something else to torment himself with.

He stared at the screen, but no slight, bedraggled figure hid in the distorted reflection of the living room. Just a tired-looking middle-aged man, who didn't look at all like Burt Reynolds to him.

Giving up, he went back to the car. The sky was still heavy and grey, but perhaps a fraction brighter than it had been.

Climbing in, he dialled through the FM bands on the radio. Nothing. None of the BBC national stations, no local commercial stations either. He switched to AM with the same result, even when he turned through the far-flung frequencies where you could usually pick up a smattering of something in French, German, Greek or various other unidentifiable languages vaguely through the hiss.

Radio black spot. Why wasn't he surprised?

If he hadn't already worked it out, Jack realised he was entirely cut off from the rest of the world. Suddenly, more than being just scared and confused, he felt terribly alone too.

# Eight

Jack made two rounds of cheese sandwiches.

"No bloody pickle," he muttered in disgust.

A cheese sandwich without pickle was an affront to both God and man. What had he been thinking when they'd bought cheese and not pickle? Actually, he knew why. He'd been far too distracted by wondering what kind of panties Moira had been wearing beneath her tight jeans as they'd sauntered hand in hand through the supermarket.

He guessed that was a question he'd never be able to answer now.

Jack felt a punch of regret and loss, sharp and sudden enough to force him to grip the side of the work surface. He screwed his eyes shut and tried not to think about what must have happened to Moira up in those dunes. He took a series of deep shuddering breaths until he had himself back under control.

He'd thought long and hard about the figure he'd seen atop Mount Dune the previous afternoon and the voice he'd heard. Had Moira been calling for help? Had the Burrows-Things erupted from the sand around her and she'd been screaming? And he'd been too bothered about getting wet to go and help her.

He didn't know. It hadn't sounded like a scream, but her

71

voice must have been raised for him to have heard it all, assuming it hadn't just been another trick of the wind and the figure he'd seen had been someone else entirely.

He told himself it had still been daylight and given the way those things had shied away from the light they probably hadn't been up and about. It was a reassurance based on little evidence, but as he had nothing else he clutched it all the same.

Jack wiped the back of his hand across his eyes and finished wrapping the sandwiches in some foil he'd found in one of the kitchen cabinets. They went into a carrier bag alongside a bottle of water and the tyre iron. The perfect seaside picnic.

Earlier he'd tried driving up the lane one more time. He was nothing if not thorough. When that had resulted in the inevitable conclusion, he'd turned the Cortina round and tried driving the other way, anticipating it would also bring him back to the House of Shells.

Instead, the lane had petered out half a mile further on, strangled by impenetrable briar thickets and dense woodland.

With no way to turn the Cortina safely around he'd driven back to the cottage in reverse.

His next bright idea had been to try and walk down the lane. Perhaps the magical mystery tour only worked if you were in a car. Nope. It had exactly the same result on foot. It just took a bit longer to get back to where he'd started from.

He'd sat on the front wall of the garden, swung his legs and tried his hand at some thinking.

Accepting, for whatever entirely implausible and messed

72

up reason, he couldn't get away from the House of Shells via the lane they'd come down, there had to be another way out.

He'd spotted no path cutting uphill through the woods; it was the same thicket of closely spaced trees and brambles the whole length of the lane, but surely there had to be another way to get off the beach? If he followed the coast one way or the other, he'd eventually find a village from where he could hire a taxi to take him to the nearest railway station. Any thought of contacting the police had long since vanished. Nobody was going to believe a damn word of this.

The sky had brightened gradually throughout the morning and the cloud was finally starting to break, allowing occasional hazy glimpses of sunlight to snick through.

If he was going to walk out, he needed to go now. He didn't want to be on that beach when the sun set.

He patted the Cortina as he passed, carrier bag swinging in his hand, in the manner of a man saying farewell to an old friend and set off down the path towards the boardwalk.

Feeling a bit like John Wayne sashaying ill-advisedly into injun country, Jack kept a wary eye on the dunes to either side of him. Big John would no doubt feel the hairs on the back of his neck prickle as the cunning natives watched him from the hills, but all Jack felt was a gnawing terror that hordes of Burrows-Things were about to erupt from the sand and haul him back to their camp for a hearty scalping.

Big John would probably be carrying some serious iron to persuade the locals to keep peaceable, but Jack somehow didn't think the tyre iron in his bag was going to do the same trick. The two cheese sandwiches even less so.

*Still, a man's gotta do...*

He kept an eye out for both the torch and Moira's jacket that he'd lost the night before, but he spotted neither from the boardwalk. He felt a tug of guilt about losing Moira's jacket up in the dunes as if he'd casually left it behind. He guessed the guilt wasn't really about the jacket, but about Moira and the nagging feeling he'd run off and abandoned her. He paused, staring up at Mount Dune, and pictured trudging up it again to search for Moira. Or, more accurately, whatever was left of her. He even went as far as pulling the tyre iron out, but he kept seeing sand-encrusted arms bursting from the ground and long clawed fingers gripping his ankle to drag him down into the lair of the Burrows-Things.

He walked swiftly on.

The Burrows were still damp from the night's rain, but the puddles had already been sucked into the sand. At least, this time, he wasn't soaked to the skin. When he'd finally peeled off his clothes after his uncomfortable soggy night locked in the Cortina, he'd found his legs had gone a bloodless shade of pale blue from the dye washed out of his jeans.

Emerging from the dunes, Jack found the tide was about halfway out and the long strip of sand was as deserted as it had been the afternoon before.

Jack sighed. He'd been sure somebody would be about. The sun was out for fuck's sake; surely some dog walker should have jumped at the chance to give Fido some exercise? You know, a nice stroll on the beach, take a ball for their loveable mutt to chase back and forth, do a bit of beachcombing, clear their lungs, help a stranger trapped by the monsters in The Burrows?

Nope, not a bit of it. Nothing. Just gulls. Still, no Burrows-Things either, so maybe he shouldn't complain too much.

He glanced back at The Burrows; Mount Dune was still easy to pick out towering over the others. He shuddered. Was whatever those things had left of Moira really still up there somewhere?

What if they hadn't killed her?

What if they were keeping her for some dark and diabolical purpose? To sacrifice at the next full moon or some other savage ritual maybe?

Jack turned around sharply and started walking down the beach.

Those things were animals, not savages. If they'd got hold of Moira they would have just…

He shook the image away. There was nothing he could do for her now.

Headlands curved around each end of the beach. A few stubborn wind-bent trees clung to the slopes here and there, but mostly it looked like gorse. Neither sported a road, building or any other sign of humanity.

Each end of the beach was book-stopped by serrated rows of rocks jutting up beneath the cliffs of the headland. The right-hand headland looked marginally lower and less precipitous than the left, which was good enough for Jack. Although he couldn't see much from here, there was surely access from the beach and a footpath leading around the headland. There were *always* footpaths; the ramblers loved a footpath and the government and National Trust duly obliged by cutting them out of the earth accordingly to encourage people to get out and "enjoy" the countryside.

He struck a diagonal path across the beach towards the sea, might as well stroll along the shoreline. As he walked, Jack noted there wasn't another set of prints on the damp sand other than his own.

*Shit, surely someone must come to this place?*

Another thing he noticed, after a while, was how clean it all was. Not a scrap of litter, not an old plastic bottle, rusting tin can or a child's forgotten toy, no jetsam or flotsam washed up on the tide line. The only things deposited by the waves churning up the beach were shells, and, frankly, he'd already seen enough of those to last a lifetime. If he ever got out of here, he was only ever taking Amanda to the mountains for holidays. She could learn to ski and bloody well like it.

*If...*

He shut that thought down. He was in Great Britain, not some godforsaken scrap of coast in Australia or Africa hundreds of miles from the nearest flushing toilet. *Nowhere* in the UK was that isolated. Even if he couldn't find a way out someone would, eventually, come here.

Hopefully, before the Burrows-Things got their hands on him.

He looked up at the sun which had already started to fall towards the west. He didn't check his watch. He was already learning to live off the land.

Besides, his stomach had started to tell him it was time for a disappointingly pickleless sandwich.

Given he hadn't brought any champagne. Jack decided to crack open the sandwiches when he got to the far end of the beach and found the path up onto the headland.

He'd been walking head down along the shoreline for twenty minutes or so, the cliffs of the headland growing closer when he saw something deposited on the beach ahead of him. It appeared to be a rock until Jack noticed it was being pushed and pulled by the surf.

His curiosity overcoming his aversion to getting wet (that really hadn't been going too well lately anyway) he let the tide wash around his boots to examine the object. It was a fish head. In fact, it was quite possibly the largest fish head Jack had ever seen.

It was roughly the size of a bicycle wheel, slightly pointed, with a small pouty mouth and bright green, not with rot or seaweed, but from scales that glimmered in the watery sunlight like burnished metal. One large yellow eye the size of a saucer stared up blankly at Jack. He assumed there was another one on the other side.

If the head was this big, what was the rest of it like? The meat around the fish's neck was pink and looked like it had been torn away.

Something even bigger had bitten its head clean off.

Jack peered out across the surf to the deeper blue-grey swells beyond and scurried away from the water's edge. He doubted anything was going to jump out of the sea to gobble him up, but, until yesterday, he wouldn't have thought any dangerous wildlife lived in sand dunes either.

Although his knowledge of fish was even more lamentable than that of birds (if you couldn't deep fry it in batter and serve it with chips he didn't really see the point of it), that fish didn't look like something that should have been swimming in the cold, murky waters off Britain. As for something big enough to eat it...

He walked on. Despite his lack of sleep, he felt oddly invigorated; his skin tingled in the breeze while the salt-infused air crackled deep in his lungs.

The beach gradually changed from pristine, uninterrupted sand to rocks. At first, just a few scattered seaweed and mussel encrusted lumps of granite peeking out of the sand, but quickly becoming bigger and more frequent, till he reached the beach's end and the rocks ran for hundreds of metres in broken lines from the dunes into the sea. Initially, only a few feet high, but incrementally getting bigger as their ranks fell back to merge into the rock face of the headland.

He picked his way through gaps in the jagged lines of black rock, clambering over the smaller ones to avoid deep pools the tide had cut into the sand at the base of some of them. The rocks were covered with barnacles, mussels, whelks and all manner of other shellfish, examples of which no doubt could be found back in the cottage. Small pools sat in cracks in the fractured rocks, choked with purple, black and green fronds of seaweed and kelp, anemones, sea urchins, crabs and tiny silver fish trapped till the next high tide.

The air was rich, briny and with the faintest hint of sulphur on the breeze. The sun was pleasantly mild, the sound of the ocean a constant deep rumble accompanied by an insistent screeching chorus from the clouds of gulls swooping down to feast along the water line.

By the time he finally clambered up upon a large flat-topped slab of rock, little shells crunching beneath his boots, he could see nothing remotely like a path. The side of the headland was rugged and broken, and any path would have involved hacking steps out of the rock, they were also unlikely to be below the high tide line. Not much point putting a path in that would be underwater twice a day.

A few little flies were buzzing around and the sulphurous smell was stronger. Something the sea had left behind was rotting down in the shadowy fissures.

He tried not to think of Moira.

After a few seconds, he pinched the bridge of his noses and blinked a couple of times before picking his way towards the dunes in search of what he was beginning to fear might be an entirely mythical path, at least at this end of the beach.

He carefully scrambled over rocks, skirting around the ones too tall or sharp-toothed to clamber over. The rocks became smaller and lighter coloured as he approached the top of the beach, interspersed with scree fields of sea-smoothed multi-hued pebbles and shattered shell remnants. He was above the normal high tide line now and the smell of rot and sulphur was stronger. The tide came less often to deposit and wash away the dead things of the sea here he supposed.

Leaving the rocks behind his boots crunched the pebbles and shell fragments underfoot. Shortly after they were back on sand as he walked in the shadow of dark, fissured cliffs, speckled with gull droppings and occasional stubborn tufts of wiry grass.

An experienced climber could probably scale it without much difficulty, plenty of little ledges and handholds were visible, but he doubted he could do it given he'd never climbed anything in his life more challenging than a flight of stairs, Mount Dune aside.

It was seventy-five to a hundred feet high by Jack's reckoning; plenty high enough to break his neck falling off it in other words.

There was clearly no access directly up to the headland from the beach. The Burrows nestled up against the cliffs, but their height meant the drop would be no more than fifty feet. And the sand was soft he supposed.

Jack found an exposed stone, grey with the remains of dead barnacles and squatted down on it. He'd found no way off the beach, but his stomach was in no mood to hang around in the hope of a celebratory sandwich. His stomach was probably a lot smarter than the rest of him.

The sandwich was dry and, inevitably, soon full of specks of sand blown by the wind. He managed one before moving on to a dessert of warm bottled water.

The dunes backed onto the Lane of Always Return, and there was no obvious way out up the densely wooded slopes without a machete; the only prospect would be a path from The Burrows up onto the headland. Which meant going back into the dunes.

He was pretty sure the Burrows-Things wouldn't be out and about in daylight from the way they'd shied from the Cortina's headlights. Still... pretty sure didn't sound like much of an endorsement to risk his life on.

But what other choice did he have?

Breaking his neck scaling the cliffs? Probably a quicker and less unpleasant death than the Burrows-Things offered, but a more certain one. And what if he didn't kill himself, but shattered his legs or broke his back? Trapped on the beach unable to move, in agony and with no prospect of help, just waiting for the sun to set and see if whatever came sniffing out of the dunes cared for the taste of sea-salted architect.

No, if he had to face those things again he wanted two legs that still worked. He filed cliff-climbing away in a box labelled *Desperate Measures of Last Resort.*

The other end of the beach was hazy with spray and mist thrown up by the incessant surf. There could be a more obvious path at that end, but the afternoon was slipping away and if he couldn't get off the beach he wanted to be in the House of Shells well before dark. There was always tomorrow.

Jack lowered his eyes and stared at his sand splattered boots. For the first time, he seriously considered the possibility he'd be spending another night here.

He'd survive it. He did last night after all.

Still, not all was lost. There were still the dunes to explore. Jack stood up, took another long swig of water and kicked sand off his boots. For a while, he just stared at the dunes. He knew it wasn't just the Burrow-Things that scared him about those dunes. There was Moira too.

What if he found her? Or, at least, what was left of her.

He didn't want to find the bloody corpse of that lovely girl, half covered in sand, the last of the summer's flies sluggishly crawling about her flat, sightless eyes. Not just for the horror of the spectacle, which was bad enough, but because then he'd *know* she was dead. Part of him still clung to the hope she might, somehow, of gotten away as unlikely as it seemed. He remembered his panic of the night before, of just wanting to run and pretend he'd never been here because of his marriage and of his job. Were they really more important things than beautiful, vivacious, sparkling Moira who, for some utterly unfathomable reason, had seen something in him that he couldn't see himself?

Worth more than her life?

She'd been in danger and all he'd thought about was running away. Ok, she was probably already dead by then, but even so. He shook his head and spat into the sand.

*Even so...*

Jack pulled the tyre iron from the bag, patted it against his leg a couple of times and then started walking towards The Burrows.

# Nine

There had been no way off the beach.

Jack had skirted the edge of The Burrows nestling beneath the cliff face all the way back till the dunes flattened out to gorse and huge walls of briar. No path. And even though the cliffs were lower, they were less weathered and shattered than the cliffs over the beach. For good measure, it also developed a pronounced overhang, just to make things that bit more difficult for him.

He'd returned to the beach and walked below The Burrows, one eye on the slopes of pale sand the other on the sun. Despite every intention of returning directly to the House of Shells, Jack found his feet reluctantly bringing him back to Mount Dune.

He didn't have time to reach the other end of the beach and explore it properly before sunset. But he could make it up Mount Dune with plenty to spare. He hoped.

He'd returned to the boardwalk and roughly followed the route he must have taken the previous evening up into the dunes. With each step into the crumbling sand, he expected to see a gnarled grotesque hand shoot upwards to grab his ankle.

His mouth dried and his heart thumped, but the sand remained motionless save for the rivulets trickling in the wake of his labouring footsteps.

Jack frequently paused to peer about him for signs of Moira, but he saw nothing, not even the jacket he'd lost when he'd tumbled down the dune the previous night.

When he reached the bottom of Mount Dune, he put his hands on his hips and glanced up at the sky. The cloud had broken to scattered remnants and the sun was falling rapidly towards the sea. He still had time. Just.

What if it was all a trick? What if the Burrows-Things were perfectly happy in daylight and had just pretended to be afraid of it to lure him back here? Moira had been up here in daylight and had never come back down again. This was stupid. Did he really expect her to be lashed to one of those ancient pieces of timber conveniently waiting his heroic rescue while the Burrows-Things pow-wowed under the sand?

No, not really.

Jack started climbing again anyway.

He didn't expect her to be there. Nothing of her that he could save anyway. But he'd run away from her twice yesterday. Or at least the possibility of her. Maybe he could have saved her if he'd headed up the dune when he'd heard her voice instead of being too worried about getting wet and too pissed at her for not being in bed with him to bother. Probably not, but he hadn't. He couldn't just... not know. If he ever escaped this place, he was going to have a long time to think about it and wonder.

Maybe in a prison cell.

Even if he could get away from here, his Cortina couldn't. He was tied to this place now and to a beautiful young woman who'd vanished. And no fool was going to believe stories about monsters living under a sand dune.

Jack's chest tightened and his breath came in quick shuddering gasps as sweat melded shirt to skin. It wasn't particularly warm, but it was a lot warmer than it had been the previous night. Without the rain and cutting wind sweat was dripping from his face long before he reached the marram crowned summit of Mount Dune.

The last few yards were torture, the marram grass left only narrow paths for him to follow between the thickening, waist-high clumps. He felt as trapped as a lab rat in a maze. His side was aching as badly as his chest while molten lead seemed to have filled his legs. He blinked away sweat, half stumbled and had to put a hand down to save himself from enjoying another face full of The Burrows.

He snatched his hand away from the sand it had sunk into.

Finally and fearfully he reached the summit and looked down into the hollow below.

The seven wooden pillars stood in their silent circle, half in shadow as the sun fell beneath the rim of the depression. The wood was bleached so white the portions still in sunlight dazzled.

No monsters were waiting for him.

Despite the things that had come bursting out into the night, inside the circle the sand was as smooth and flat as plaster again. Free of any detritus or grass it stood out starkly against the marram grass choked sand around it. There was no sound save the wind and Jack's own ragged breathing.

In daylight, the "caldera" looked like it had been lifted cleanly out of the top of the dune with a giant ice cream scoop.

When no horde of Burrows-Things came hollering towards him, Jack stuck the tyre iron in his belt and drained his water bottle in big noisy gulps. For a moment, he had the manic urge to hurl the empty bottle into the pristine sand within the wooden circle. Like fresh snow, it begged to be messed up a bit.

However, he decided he needed the bottle to fill up from the tap in the cottage. Besides, he didn't want to rile the locals too much. As with the beach, he hadn't seen one scrap of rubbish desecrating the sand. None of the crap that soiled every other beach Jack had ever visited. Not a crisp bag, not a sweet wrapper, not a drink can, not even a faded ice lolly stick plonked into the soft sand as a memorial to a day by the sea. Maybe the locals didn't take kindly to litterbugs.

There was no sign of Moira either. No sign of anything much but grass and sand and those seven ancient sun-whitened pillars.

Jack slowly circled the rim of Mount Dune. This was as close as he intended to get to those wooden pillars and what lay beneath them. Tyre iron hanging by his side he picked his way around the marram grass as best he could. The previous night's rain had washed the sand, but if someone had died up here - died, violently and horribly - wouldn't there still be some sign of it? Could the rain have washed away every trace of blood, or would there still be a darker stain to signify where...

Jack looked sharply away and swallowed.

Mount Dune was, at least, a third higher than any of the other dunes making up The Burrows and it offered a magnificent view of the beach, curving in a crescent between the two headlands, as well as the rest of the undulating grass-topped dune field. To the west, the low autumn sun had turned the sea into a sheet of restless quicksilver that dazzled his eyes. To the east, it had set the autumnal reds and golds of the rusting trees upon the hillside afire.

The world was bathed in the honeyed light of the falling sun. Nothing moved but the grass, seabirds and the ever-restless sea. The clouds had broken into a myriad of shapes and forms tumbling across the sky and those to the west were already fringed with gold.

Despite everything Jack could do nothing but stand and stare, letting the beauty of the place wash over him before moving on to circle the rim.

Several times he stopped to scan the view, not just looking for Moira, but for signs of anyone. There was nothing. Not on the beach, The Burrows, the headlands or the thickly wooded hills rising sharply inland. He could see no trace of humanity in any direction other than the distant chimneys of the House of Shells. Not a building, not a wall, not a telegraph pole, not a pylon, not a road, not even a ship or a boat or a yacht somewhere out towards the blinding horizon. Nothing. Jack hadn't thought places like this still existed. Completely untouched by the presence of man. For fuck's sake, it was 1980, someone must come here!

He looked up at the sky. He hadn't even seen or heard a plane or helicopter.

He spotted the thick ridge of marram grass he'd ran into

when he'd been blundering through the darkness with the Burrows-Things in pursuit. If he'd gone the other way, he would only have gotten past it by going down onto the beach, where he would have had the Burrows-Things between him and the House of Shells.

If he hadn't followed the lilting laughter of the Giggle-finch...

Jack stopped.

What the hell had that been? The disembodied giggling he'd heard several times. A ghost?

It was a ridiculous thought. One he would have laughed heartily at before he'd seen with his own eyes that the world was a much stranger place than he'd ever imagined.

What if it had been Moira? Her ghost trying to save him. She'd died up here and her spirit had led him safely back to the House of Shells? That figure he'd seen reflected only in the blank TV screen, a young woman with long dark hair. Could that have been Moira?

He almost expected to hear a playful giggle in his ear, but the only sound was the sighing of the wind. He shivered all the same.

Jack walked on. Pushing the thought from his head and feeling foolish for even considering it. He could see nothing of Moira, no trace she'd ever been here. The Burrows stretched away around him. Mount Dune was the best vantage point, but the undulating dunes could have hidden a hundred bodies from his view.

On the landward side of the dune, his shadow stretched out across the undulating hills of sand, alien and elongated. He raised his arm and a spindly too-long shadow reached out across the gently swaying crowns of grass.

"Moira..." Jack called as if she might still be out there, wandering dazed and confused somewhere in that rolling, crumpled landscape of mounded sand and restless grass.

"MOIRA!!!" He screamed, shocked by both the sound of his voice breaking the silence and the pain twisting and crackling within that one simple word.

MOIRA!!!" He bellowed, almost bending double with the effort to propel her name from this body.

Distantly a gull screamed.

No other sound came in reply bar his own stifled sob.

# Ten

*Bread, milk, bacon (half a pack), baked beans (two tins), pork sausages (8), mushrooms, tomatoes, apples, onions, tea, sugar, cornflakes, butter, dried pasta, crisps (salt and vinegar x 2, prawn cocktail x 2), beer (8).*

Jack had spread the groceries over the noticeably wobbly kitchen table and made a list in the hope there might seem more if he wrote it all down. He thought it was prudent to see how much he had to live off. And how long it might last.

Had they expected this to keep them going for three nights?

Jack scratched his head. Well, they had the car, there would have been pub lunches, fish and chips out of a bag somewhere, maybe watching the sunset over the sea, Moira dipping in to steal the best-looking chips when-

The hiss of the opening beer can cut the thought off. He was trying not to think about Moira with a complete lack of success.

After taking a mouthful, he scrubbed out the 8 after beer and replaced it with a 7.

Two plain and rather flimsy wooden chairs sat either side of the round table covered with a faded red and white checked tablecloth. The second chair was, obviously, empty and Jack couldn't help but stare. Imagining Moira hunched over it, wolfing down her breakfast. Fry ups. They were going to have a fry up every morning and be damned, she'd announced as they'd cosied up in the corner of a pub planning this little adventure a couple of weeks before.

"Never mind the calories, you'll be getting plenty of exercise…" she'd told him with a theatrical wink and a nudge of the elbow.

And she'd been right too. He'd had loads of exercise. Just not the kind he'd anticipated.

While poor Moira had probably ended up being eaten *for* breakfast.

The disturbingly maniacal giggle he was starting to get far too familiar with spurted from between his lips again.

"Not fucking funny…"

After putting his larder away, Jack carried the beer into the front room and slumped onto the sofa, which he'd earlier dragged in front of the locked and bolted door.

Moira's duffel lay in the corner of the room. He'd had to move it when he shifted the sofa and he'd felt guilty just putting a hand on it.

All the little things of her life she'd never touch again.

She might not be dead. He kept telling himself it was possible given he'd found no trace of her up in The Burrows. He'd managed to run away from those monsters and Moira was, after all, younger, fitter and a lot, lot smarter than he was.

Maybe she'd gotten away, maybe she'd found a way off the beach. She was a local after all. Maybe she went to get help and maybe she'd even managed to avoid getting locked up in an asylum.

Jack sipped his beer and continued staring at the duffel.

Yeah, maybe.

It'd taken him a while to decide where to try and hide out the night. The Cortina was, obviously, mobile and its headlights seemed to scare the beasties away, but it would be a long night cramped in the car staring into the darkness.

The House of Shells had sturdy thick wooden doors back and front, each with a deadbolt and two hefty metal bolts top and bottom. The windows had no shutters unfortunately and would take only a rock to smash. However, another door at the top of the stairs could be bolted and barricaded.

There were also powerful external patio lights back and front he somehow hadn't noticed before as well as the internal lights. Hopefully, that would keep them back in the shadows. He considered leaving the Cortina's lights on for added illumination but decided he didn't want to kill the battery if he needed to get away from the house. Ok, he wouldn't get far, but they hadn't wanted to follow him down the lane last night.

The fact the House of Shells might have a ghost he could only see in the TV screen shouldn't form part of his calculation. He probably hadn't seen anything anyway...

However, there was one final difference that swung his decision towards staying in the house. The Cortina didn't have curtains. He really didn't want to have to see those God awful ugly fuckers again.

The curtains were drawn back and front, which he somehow found more reassuring than the bolted doors. He'd taken a couple of chairs from the dinner table in the back room, which were heftier than the ones at the little kitchen table, and wedged one against the back door and taken another up to the landing so he could wedge that one shut too.

He'd searched the house for weapons but had come up with only an old wooden mallet, a broom and a collection of uniformly blunt kitchen knives. He liked the idea of making a spear of some kind with gaffer tape he had in the boot of the car. It seemed suitably Robinson Crusoe and might allow him to keep some distance between himself and any Burrows-Thing he had to deal with. Sadly, all of the knives in the kitchen drawer would struggle to cut even the bread he had. Fortunately, that was pre-sliced, nobody had only bad luck after all.

He'd slipped the mallet into his belt. It was a tad uncomfortable, but it saved him from putting it down and not having a weapon if he needed one. The tyre iron still felt his best bet though and he'd stuck it into his belt too, which had made him feel slightly more John Wayne. At least until it slipped out of his belt, narrowly missed his foot and made him jump back with a startled yelp as it clattered to the floor.

After that, he just carried it in his free hand.

The darkness was pushing in on the House of Shells; Jack could feel it, like pressure on his eyelids. There was silence outside, even the gulls seemed to have gotten bored and gone somewhere else.

Back up on the darkened Burrows, he wondered if things were starting to pull themselves out of the sand yet.

\*

Jack had retreated upstairs once he'd finished his beer. He decided to leave the rest in the fridge. One beer, under the circumstances, was a small treat he felt he deserved (there weren't many others on offer), but to get completely shit-faced would have been stupid.

Very tempting, but still stupid.

The water they'd brought with them was gone, but he'd kept both plastic bottles and he refilled them from the tap. He'd expected the water to taste stale and metallic, but in fact, it was cold, refreshing and sweet. Far better than what came out of his tap back in London. Score one for the Holiday from Hell at last.

He knew he should take food upstairs, he was bound to get hungry and once he was bolted in upstairs, he didn't want to come down again. Luckily, he'd found a bucket under the stairs, which took care of the only other reason he'd have for venturing down.

In the end, he settled for a couple of apples, another cheese sandwich, a bag of crisps (prawn cocktail, the salt and vinegar ones had been for Moira) and a can of beans.

A full and hearty meal.

Well, when you gotta live off the land.

He'd have a proper breakfast tomorrow. A fry up for Moira to celebrate still being alive. If that wasn't being too presumptuous of course.

Provisions and tyre iron in hand, Jack had a last scoot around the downstairs to ensure, once more, he'd locked everything that could be locked and left on every available light source. The energy crisis could go screw itself.

Finally, he eyed Moira's duffel. He wasn't sure if leaving it where it was or taking it upstairs would make him feel more guilty. In the end, he decided to be practical, there might be something useful in it. A machine gun was top of his wish list, but he wasn't overly hopeful Moira had been that kind of girl.

Had been.

Shit, he was already thinking of her in the past tense.

He scooped up the duffel and lumbered upstairs for the long night ahead.

\*

Things were moving beyond the reach of the lights.

Burrows-Things.

Jack had promised himself he wouldn't look out of the window unless it was absolutely necessary. It had taken twenty minutes of restless pacing before he started twitching the curtain like an old lady with too much time on her hands.

Nothing seemed to be happening at the back where the dark woods loomed over the House of Shell's garden, but out the front, beyond the lane amongst the gorse bushes and scattered whitebeams, monsters were about.

Monsters with a hankering for a little piggy dinner.

He didn't have a house of straw, sticks or bricks to hide in. This little piggy had a house of shells and Jack had no real idea how it would stand up if the monsters started huffing and puffing.

Jack put his face to the glass and cupped his hands against the light reflecting off the pane. The sky still held the faintest blush in the west and the cloud had scattered to intermittently reveal a near full moon.

There were, at least, a dozen of them though it was hard to be sure as they stuck to the darkest shadows beyond the reach of the patio lights. Some might just be windblown branches swaying back and forth, but others were too purposeful. A couple of times the shadows detached themselves from the greater dark and scurried in the open; tall, gangling, awkward shadows. Sometimes they gathered in little knots, like schoolboys whispering mischief to each other.

None ventured into the pool of light thrown by the House of Shells, however, and Jack took some comfort from that. If they decided they weren't so scared of a couple of light bulbs, after all, he doubted his makeshift barricades, tyre iron and gnarled old mallet with a slightly wobbly head would keep them out until sunrise.

Maybe he should have stayed in the Cortina.

Still, too late now.

He let the curtain fall back and paced some more. Now and then he heard them howling and gibbering. Maybe at him, maybe at the moon. He didn't know. Each time he scurried back to the window, his heart thumping wildly, and peered out, expecting to see them edging closer, egging each other on to brave the light, but each time they were still clustered in the trees. No closer than they had been the last time he'd checked.

After a couple of hours, Jack found terror was subsiding slowly into boredom. It seemed more than slightly surreal to be perched on the edge of a bed, eating a sandwich consisting of dry bread and sweaty cheese in between dipping into a bag of crisps while barricaded inside a house surrounded by monsters.

Still, he was hungry.

And he wished he'd brought another beer up. It felt like it was going to be a long night.

*

God, he was tired.

His eyes were heavy, his body ached and he reeked of well past its best sweat. His ribs had started to throb again as well. He wanted to sleep, but a part of him, the irritating, paranoid part he guessed, kept whispering that as soon as he went to sleep the Burrows-Things would rush the house, force their way in and devour him before he could even grab his trusty tyre iron.

Maybe they would. After all, his knowledge of monsters was even more lamentable than his knowledge of birds and fish.

He kept pacing, eyeing the two beds like they were coquettish little vixens trying to lure him into their wicked clutches. He knew, however, he wasn't going to be able to stay awake all night. If the Burrows-Things were actually doing something, then the adrenaline rush of terror might keep him going till dawn, but simply lurking really wasn't going to cut the mustard.

He needed something to occupy his mind. He'd brought two paperbacks, but for some reason, they didn't appeal anymore. In the circumstances neither Stephen King's *The*

*Shining* nor James Herbert's *The Rats* made the best bedtime reading.

His eye fell on Moira's duffel. The TV and radio didn't work here, but she'd probably brought her cassette player and some tapes. He'd never really understood her taste in music, but it was better than silence. And with any luck the *Sex Pistols* and *New York Dolls* would scare the bejesus out of the Burrows-Things. They'd pretty much had that effect on him when he'd first heard Moira play them after all.

Feeling only slightly like a thief and voyeur Jack hoisted Moira's bag onto the bed, loosened the drawstrings and pulled the top open. The first thing he found staring up at him was her *Ramones* t-shirt.

He pulled it out and held it in his hands. Faded black, worn and washed to a downy softness, it was too large and shapeless for such a pretty girl as Moira. The tatty and scratched photo of four long-haired oiks in leather jackets on the front wasn't particularly flattering either.

She'd looked unutterably beautiful when she'd worn it.

With a hesitant and shaking hand he raised it to his face and breathed through the fabric. Her scent was so strong it was almost as if she was in the room with him, arms hooked around his neck, that wicked, mischievous grin kinking her lips, misty grey eyes, wide and expectant.

Almost…

Outside a Burrow-thing wailed; a long, mournful lament that seemed to be full of wretched sadness and loss rather than slavering, hungry menace.

Had he loved her?

He'd been thrilled, excited, intoxicated by her. He'd been swept along by her lust for life like a torrent of white water bursting upon an unsuspecting desert canyon. He'd been aroused and flattered and intrigued by her. His life had become a barren, joyless repetition. Walking the same circles, locked into grooves of conformity and expectation. She'd taken his hand and shown him something different.

Or maybe he was just a middle-aged man having a tawdry, meaningless affair with a younger woman. Which wasn't particularly different at all. It happened the world over. Had since man first walked the earth and would continue till he breathed his last. But it hadn't felt like that. It had felt wondrous.

Had he loved her?

Jack curled up on the bed, Moira's t-shirt still clutched to his face, his throat thickening as his eyes stung. Whatever it had been, it had been more than just sex. He'd been happy. For the first time in so long, he'd been happy. And now she was dead and he was trapped here with nothing but her old t-shirt and the ghost of her scent for company.

Out in the darkness that enveloped the House of Shells, more Burrows-Things started yowling and baying in a doleful, melancholy serenade.

# Eleven

Jack sat and stared at the cliffs, elbows on his knees, chin in his hands. Every now and then he turned his head slightly to the right so he could sniff his fingers.

He was squatting on a desk-sized slab of rock jutting from the sand. It had a convenient and posterior friendly smooth top. The tide had sculpted a shallow basin around it which trapped seawater as the tide retreated; at the bottom of the pool, a grit of finely ground shell remnants and small rounded pebbles coated the sand. Jack had taken off his boots and socks to dangle his feet in the water, occasionally pushing his toes deep into the gooey sand and wiggling them. His eyes didn't leave the cliffs towering above him.

From a distance, they'd looked uniformly black, but up close he could see all manner of subtle hues in the dark rock; ferrous-reds, earthy-browns, olive-greens, burnt-ochres. Here and there jagged veins of brilliant white forked through it. In places, there was an almost golden sheen glimmering softly in the sunlight. No doubt if he'd known anything about geology he could guess at what minerals were responsible for each colour. But, Jack was realising, there were an awful lot of subjects he knew absolutely nothing about.

How to find a path being chief amongst them.

He'd walked down to the left-hand side of the beach that morning to explore, technically he supposed it was the southern end, but as no one was around to contradict him he guessed he could call it whatever he damned well liked.

The sky was mostly clear and it was pleasantly mild in the sunshine, though when a stray cloud did cover the sun, the temperature dropped noticeably enough for Jack to scramble to zip up his coat. He'd swung the carrier bag with his sandwich, water and tyre iron in it like a child going to school. A child hopefully dreaming it would be his last day at school.

Jack was convinced there had to be a way out. He was also convinced he'd bump into another human being at some point too. So far, he'd been proved wrong on both counts.

He'd been woken by the sound of murderous shrieking outside the bedroom window. He was sitting up clutching the tyre iron before he'd realised the awful cawing screech was just a gull perched on the window ledge rather than a Burrows-Thing. It had made for an effective wake-up call, all the same.

The sun was up and he'd slept long and dreamlessly curled up on the bed, still clutching Moira's *Ramones* t-shirt. Despite the rude awakening he felt well rested. It usually took an indulgently long shower, numerous cups of coffee and several hours to shrug off the final tendrils of sleep, but by the time he'd reached the bottom of the stairs he was wide awake and brimming with uncommon energy. He felt bright-eyed and bushy of tail. Even the pain in his side seemed to have gone.

Tyre iron to hand he'd explored the cottage and found everything as he'd left it, then dragged the sofa away from the front door and checked outside. Nothing seemed out of place with either the house or the car. If the Burrows-Things had been up to any mischief, beyond their strange cackles and wails, there was no sign of it.

It was still cool enough in the early dawn light to steam his breath, but despite shivering he'd checked across the lane where the Burrows-Things had huddled and watched the House of Shells from.

The soil here was well laced with sand anyway, but there were smatterings atop the wiry grass too. There was also a smell; dry, rich, pungent. Like meat cured in the sun. It came and went as he moved about the trees and presumably marked where the Burrows-Things had gathered. It wasn't an entirely unpleasant aroma – he'd regularly smelt far worse on the London Underground – but he'd been simultaneously repulsed and fascinated by it. The smell was strongest by the trees and he'd let his hand absently stroke the bark as he breathed in the heady scent.

In the end, the cold and his stomach got the better of him and he returned to the House of Shells.

Whatever the Burrows-Things smelt of, his stink was probably far worse and he took a shower, which was surprisingly hot and powerful, before having the fry up he'd promised himself for surviving the night. In truth, survival hadn't been particularly challenging. Boredom being the only actual threat, but still, a promise was a promise. Especially when it was made to your stomach.

Sausage, bacon, a couple of fried eggs, beans, mushrooms and tomatoes. Toast and tea. But no tomato ketchup. They'd seriously cocked up with the condiments.

Still, after demolishing breakfast, with only the vague nagging doubt that maybe he should be rationing his food, Jack felt enormously better.

He'd left his plate on the table and the pans on the stove in the certain knowledge he would be saying goodbye to the House of Shells for the last time.

That had been the plan anyway.

*

The southern cliffs were identical to those at the other end of the beach. Only bigger.

There was no path up them, either from the beach or off The Burrows, which led back to the lane. Again, there was no sign of humanity. By Jack's calculation, the road he and Moira had driven down before turning onto the lane should be just over the cliffs, but he heard no murmur of traffic from the rest of the world. The exit from the lane onto the road should be only a little further down from where he'd emerged from The Burrows. However, he could see nothing but the lane stretching away into the distance till it merged with the trees on either side and knew walking that way would only take him back to the House of Shells.

Instead, he'd skirted the edge of The Burrows beneath the multi-hued cliffs and returned to the beach. He didn't hold much hope of finding another way off the beach, but the constant rhythmic pounding of the surf might help him think.

103

He walked bare-footed, lacing the boots together and slinging them over his shoulder. Despite worrying a Burrow's-Thing's hand might burst from the ground at any moment, he liked the feel of the sand on his feet. The silky dry kind that made up The Burrows and upper beach which held the warmth of the day, as well as the soft, wet squishy stuff below the tide line, teased and carved into undulating ripples by the ebb and flow of the sea.

Jack meandered down to the surf, whistling something tuneless. The waves were smaller today and the wind lighter, in the sunshine the sea was an undulant mosaic of blue-greys and aquamarines topped with ribbons of white from the ranks of tumbling waves galloping shoreward.

The water was cold around his ankles, but not unpleasantly so. Occasionally, a larger wave would arrive, the spray doting the jeans he'd rolled, rather unfetchingly he supposed, above his knees. He thought about just taking them off, it wasn't as if anybody was around to be traumatised by the sight of a middle-aged man paddling in his y-fronts, but, in the end, he settled for simply staring out to sea.

Could he swim around either of the headlands?

He'd been a decent swimmer once and had gone to the pool a few times a week for years before he'd got married, but he couldn't remember the last time he'd been. The water here was cold, the sea about the headlands full of jutting, jagged rocks surrounded by all manner of currents that might throw him onto them or sweep him out to sea. In all likelihood, it would be a surer way of killing himself than trying to scale the cliffs.

Still, the thought of jumping into the water was suddenly appealing. He could swim out a bit, he was sure he could go a couple of hundred yards out safely enough and swim back to shore with the waves. It would give him another view of the beach, headlands and the wooded hills, burning from green to russet with the chill autumn nights, rising beyond the lane and the House of Shells. He hadn't brought a towel, but-

Jack froze.

Someone was walking down the beach towards him.

"Oh, thank fucking God!"

A stout woman in a sensible green coat was ambling along the shoreline with a golden retriever (dogs he could name) bouncing in and out of the surf. As Jack watched, the dog shook its coat and presented something to the woman. A yellow ball, which she duly hurled back into the waves for the dog, tail beating frantically, to bound after.

"Hey!" Jack shouted, suddenly immensely grateful he'd decided against stripping down to his y-fronts.

Jack splashed out of the sea and started running towards the woman, waving and calling, his jeans slowly unrolling as he pounded across the sand. His boots were thudding against his back and chest and he clawed them off to carry in the same hand as his bag, leaving the other one free for throwing around above his head as if he were drowning.

She didn't seem to be paying him much attention. As he drew closer, he could see she looked like the kind of redoubtable, practical woman not likely to be much put out by madmen shouting at her and waving their arms about. However much underwear they were displaying.

Jack slowed down as he approached her, she was still staring at her dog, a little smile on her face, iron-grey hair fell neatly to her collar from beneath the kind of flat beige hat beloved by country folk who enjoyed shooting the wildlife.

He skidded to a halt, his heels digging into the wet sand. He dropped both his boots and the carrier bag. Jack felt his mouth flapping about, but nothing much was coming out. Nothing vaguely comprehensible anyway.

He could see straight through the woman.

The rocks and cliffs at the far end of the beach were clearly visible, tinged green by her coat, but there never the less. As she stooped to retrieve her dog's ball something else dawned on him. He couldn't hear anything. The woman's mouth moved as she spoke to the retriever, but no sound came out. The dog barked in reply, equally silently, before shaking his coat and sending droplets of seawater cascading in all directions. The woman pulled a face as the water splattered over her. Those that reached Jack passed straight through him.

Then the woman turned sharply and walked straight through him too.

There was no sensation, nothing at all.

He watched her march off along the beach, seeing the cliffs ripple along with her sensible coat, before realising the dog wasn't following her. He was sitting with the ball at his feet staring at Jack, tongue lolling out as he panted, head cocked slightly to one side.

"Can you see me?"

The dog barked, silently.

Jack squatted down and reached for the ball. There was nothing there. His eyes were telling him there was a ball, albeit a faintly translucent one, but he felt nothing till his fingers touched the wet sand.

The dog barked again, jumped away from Jack before returning to snatch up the ball in his mouth and sprinting after his mistress.

Jack started to trot after them. His mind was freewheeling again and no actual thoughts were forming.

"Hey!" he shouted, "Help me! *Please!*"

She looked like the kind of woman who would know exactly what to do in any given situation, from a disappointing soufflé to the end of the world. Unfortunately, she was utterly unaware Jack was shouting in her ear.

She was getting fainter, both the woman and dog slowly fading as if consumed by an encroaching mist. The retriever gave him a last curious glance over his shoulder, ball still clamped in his mouth, and then they were gone.

Jack looked up and down the beach. The only footprints in the smooth wet sand were his.

Jack's legs buckled and he found himself sitting in the wet sand turned to a mirror by the film of water on its surface. For a minute or two he stared dumbly at the reflections of the clouds and sky while the seat of his jeans soaked up seawater. He didn't quite know what to say or do or even think.

After all, it was only the second time he'd seen a ghost.

# Twelve

The House of Shells was a holiday let.

He wasn't sure why this simple fact hadn't dawned on him before. A combination of grief, terror, disorientation and general befuddlement Jack supposed.

At some point the owners would come to tidy up, make sure nothing had been stolen or damaged and generally make the place ready for the next set of guests stupid enough to want to holiday at Hell-on-Sea.

It struck him as he walked back down the Lane of Always Return. He was taking the long way back by not heading away from the House of Shells, rechecking the bramble thickets for a path, or at least a thin patch where he might be able to penetrate a few yards without being torn to shreds. He wasn't having any luck.

He walked with a fallen branch he'd press-ganged into service as a makeshift staff to poke and thrash the undergrowth with. As he ambled, his mind turned to who else might come to the House of Shells. The cottage seemed to be connected to the mains electricity; there was gas and water too. The postman must drop by to deliver bills and other sundry junk mail. If they could get in, how come they could get out? As he hadn't stumbled across any skeletons wearing a postman's hat at a jaunty angle, he assumed they could.

So why not him?

He didn't know. But the thought someone must eventually come to the house lifted his spirits. Though there'd better come quick as he was due home tomorrow evening.

The thought of Amanda shining the desk lamp in his eyes and demanding to know where he'd been – she was a woman who definitely had ways of making people talk – didn't fill him with quite as much dread as a horde of jabbering Burrows-Things. But she wasn't far behind.

Still, he had a few days before she got back from her mother in Spain, where the old bird, a woman for whom the word *brassy* was entirely inadequate, thankfully flew every year as soon as the mercury started falling.

Amanda would phone home once he was due back from his "conference," and would want to know why he wasn't picking up. Maybe she'd call the office if she couldn't get hold of him at home. Jack winced and tried to push his wife from his mind. One problem at a time.

Jack pulled his right hand from his pocket and absent-mindedly sniffed his fingers as he walked. He'd been doing it on and off throughout the day without a great deal of thought. Another nervous tick he was developing. Still, better than maniacal giggling.

The sun was draping the lane in diffuse, dappled light through the reddening foliage. Birds were singing and a few darted across the path ahead of him as he strolled. They seemed happy enough at least.

Another thought struck him. He seemed to be on a roll. The lane might only be two narrow ruts primarily designed to punish a car's suspension, but it was clear of weeds and other encroaching growth other than a dusting of autumn leaves. He didn't know much about plants, but he knew they liked to grow. He knew because his garden was full of bloody weeds. It certainly wasn't through traffic keeping the lane from being reclaimed by the woods and briars. Someone must be hacking them back reasonably frequently.

He continued to run an eye along the wooded slope as he walked, several times pausing to investigate a thinner patch of vegetation, but he was never able to penetrate more than a couple of yards before becoming enclosed by brambles and briars that tore at his clothes and nicked his exposed hands.

The House of Shells was almost within sight when he noticed a sliver of a gap between two bramble thickets partially obscured by a tree. Pulling his coat sleeve over his hand, he pushed some of the grasping spiteful branches back and found, for once, the gap between the brambles widened into something that might, with a charitable frame of mind, be described as a path.

The day was drawing to a close, but Jack reckoned he still had enough time to explore a little further.

The path rose sharply between the briars and the ground was churned to cloying mud, causing him to slip several times as he scrambled excitedly upwards. This had to go somewhere, didn't it?

Over the hills and far away, hopefully.

Another giggle squirmed past his lips before he could choke it.

The sun was setting behind him, the reddening light mellowed by the overhanging branches and briars towering on either side of him. A little wind had picked up, enough to rustle the surrounding foliage. Like a beast starting to rouse itself as a little piggy foolishly clambered into its maws.

Jack eyed the briars on either side, rising half as high above him. He told himself sternly they were not going to snap shut on him. They were *just* briars after all.

After a couple of minutes further slipping and sliding as he used his makeshift staff to battle up the slope, the briars unexpectedly parted on either side of him. The slope flattened out to reveal a shadowy clearing amidst a towering ring of briars and overarching trees.

Jack stood, resting on his staff and panting. The clearing was roughly circular and almost entirely filled by a pond fringed with bulrushes and thick with water lilies, the snow-white flowers already closing against the coming night.

Once he'd caught his breath, Jack carefully circled the pond, there were a few feet between the water's edge and the encroaching briars, which presented an impenetrable thicket around the still water. The path up from the lane was the only way in or out of the clearing.

"Fuck it..."

Jack leant on his staff and stared at the velvet dark water between the lilies. Dragonflies flitted across the pond, silent and iridescent in the shadowy light.

He shivered and did up his coat, shielded from the sun it was cold enough for his breath to steam a little. Not that the dragonflies seemed particularly bothered. Wasn't this too chilly for insects, particularly such big ones? Flowering water lilies too for that matter. In late October? Jack shrugged. The list of things he knew nothing about...

Despite his disappointment at finding nothing but a dead end in reward for scratched hands and muddy jeans, the pond was so tranquil all Jack wanted to do was stare and find his troubles and woes diminishing like a hitchhiker in a rear-view mirror. Somebody else's problem.

If it hadn't been so chilly Jack would have squatted down by the pond to watch the dragonflies and lily pads. The air was coolly moist and seemed honeyed by the scent of a million exotic flowers, rather than few dozen unoccasional flowering water lilies

Jack heaved himself around and begun to move back to the muddy little path through the briars when a flicker of movement caught his eye.

A pair of butterflies were fluttering over the thick bull rushes on the opposite side of the pond, but they were like no butterflies Jack had ever seen, each wing was only a fraction smaller than his outstretched hand and a shimmering, translucent gold shot through with gossamer veins of black. The golden wings were catching the sun to glow and sparkle as if diamonds were trapped in their beating wings.

Except no sunlight fell on them.

The clearing was deep in shadow, the setting sun shielded from the pond by the giant tangled walls of brambles and the trees rising above them.

Jack watched entranced as the two butterflies cavorted around each other, like teasing lovers darting out of each other's grasp with lilting giggles and sparkling eyes. They drifted across the pond in their own peculiar pool of radiance. Jack raised his head as they flew above him and

112

up over the brambles. He blinked and told himself he hadn't really seen the momentary sparky trails of golden light fizzing in the wake of their beating wings.

Once they'd disappeared over the thickets, he was pretty sure he'd imagined both their ethereal glow and the trails of liquid gold fading behind them. What he couldn't put down to imagination was what the hell were two such enormous butterflies doing here. Maybe they got that big in the Amazon, but not here. Perhaps they'd escaped from a zoo?

Jack returned to the path and made his way back down towards the lane.

He wondered if the Burrows-Things had escaped from a zoo too...

*

He arrived back at the House of Shells no wiser than when he'd left it. He was surprised to see how low the sun was in the sky and glanced at his watch. Home safely before sunset, but only just. He blinked. His watch and his reading of the sun's position in the sky couldn't both be wrong, but where had his day gone? He hadn't spent that long staring into the lily pond... had he?

He drank the last of the water standing by his trusty Cortina, staring out through the trees towards The Burrows and the summit of Mount Dune, stark against the lowering sun.

*Was Moira still up there somewhere?*

Even after revisiting Mount Dune he didn't know for sure, but she must either be dead in the sand somewhere or she'd run far, far away after coming across those awful things. He

113

hoped with all his heart it was the latter, but he didn't think so. He didn't think so at all.

He missed her so damn much. Strange he should not even realise just how much he cared about her until...

Jack blinked and looked around him.

He'd wandered back into the trees without even really noticing his feet were moving. Back to where the scent of the Burrows-Things still hung in the air, musky and pungent, clinging and cloying.

It smelt even stronger than it had in the morning and it left him feeling light-headed as he absently stroked the tree bark, enjoying the roughness scraping his fingertips, exploring the ridges, fissures and cracks as if it were some bizarre alien landscape rather than merely a tree.

Jack shook his head. He'd been alone too long if he was getting this fond of a tree. The sun had fallen behind the dunes and their shadows stretched out far enough to caress the House of Shells. How long had he been stroking bark?

He turned around and hurried back towards the cottage.

There was another night to prepare for and he'd no time to spare molesting trees.

\*

After Jack had changed out of the latest set of clothes he'd managed to soak and despoil he locked and bolted the front door and dragged the sofa back across. He didn't expect the Burrows-Things to try and break in, but he wasn't going to take anything for granted. He then checked all the lights. He hadn't found any spare bulbs in the cottage and the thought of the lights popping one by one to leave him huddled in the darkness was a nagging worry.

Once the House of Shells was fortified to his satisfaction, he lay on the sofa and stared at the ceiling for a while, listening to the gulls and imagining the sun falling beneath the sea.

He jerked his head a few times to stay awake.

The combination of unfamiliar exercise and the almost as unfamiliar clean air was leaving him bone weary, but he didn't want to nod off now. He felt safer upstairs, plus he needed to eat.

Tossing ideas about what gastronomic marvel he could throw together, he sauntered into the kitchen stifling a yawn which quickly morphed into a frown.

His breakfast things were neatly piled on the drainer by the sink.

Hadn't he just walked out and left everything? He thought he had, in fact, he was damn sure he had. Washing up had always been something he'd avoided and when Amanda was away, the plates tended to amalgamate into one huge congealing conglomerate of crockery, cutlery and pans festering in the sink.

He picked up a plate he'd left smeared with breakfast grease to harden on the kitchen table. Now it radiated TV commercial glinty cleanness. It certainly didn't look like his handiwork. But he must have done it. Just too stressed out and traumatised to remember.

*Shit.* He'd become so fucked up he'd developed some kind of domestic chore amnesia...

Jack slapped a pan onto the stove and eventually conjured up something reasonably edible (given the low

115

starting expectations) from the pasta, onions and mushroom with a bit of cheese grated over the top, followed by an apple for dessert.

Afterwards, he stared at his dwindling larder. Maybe not such a big fry up for breakfast tomorrow. After filling his water bottles, he hit all the lights and retreated upstairs to lock himself in for another night, the detritus of his cooking abandoned behind him.

He stopped midway up the stairs. The sand was gone.

The little piles sprinkled over the steps when he'd been out looking for Moira that first night had all vanished.

He was pretty sure he hadn't washed up after breakfast. He was absolutely positive he hadn't taken a broom to the stairs.

Someone giggled again.

Jack jumped and almost lost his footing on the stairs.

He rushed back downstairs – the giggle had definitely come from down there – but found nothing out of place.

"Moira..."

The cottage was silent. In ghost stories, the hero would often sense some otherworldly presence, the temperature would fall, the hairs on the back of their necks would stand up, they'd be some undefinable wrongness, but Jack's senses were telling him nothing other than he'd undercooked the onions in his pasta.

It wasn't Moira. Why would her ghost be giggling and laughing? Besides he'd heard the giggle for the first time just a few minutes after Moira had run off towards The Burrows when he'd been ditching the groceries in the kitchen. It didn't work like that with ghosts. Did it?

"Who are you?"

Jack kept glancing at the TV screen, but the only reflection was of himself pacing a slow circle about the living room. No answer came.

"I don't suppose you know a way off the beach, do you?"

Jack moved through to the kitchen, his dinner things were still spread about as he left them.

"Are you a ghost? Or something else?"

There would have been a time when trying to have a conversation with a disembodied giggle would have been both surreal and ludicrous. And that time had been a little more than two days ago. But now, what the hell...

"Thank you for helping me out on The Burrows the other night, if I'd carried on the way I'd been heading..."

Whatever the Giggle-finch was, she wasn't a great conversationalist. When no answers, or even further giggles, were forthcoming Jack retreated upstairs and barricaded himself in once more. However, he found she was excellent at making up a bed. After staring at the precisely folded sheets and plumped up pillows he'd left crumpled and askew that morning he decided he'd sleep in the other bedroom.

He thought of the back bedroom as the White Room, given the colour of pretty much everything in it, from the bed frame to a whitewashed chest of draws (all empty), to a wicker chair, to the walls and bedside table. The sheets and blankets were white, the curtains were white. Someone liked white. Unlike the other rooms of the cottage, the White Room didn't have sketches and drawings of shells adorning the walls. It had paintings of them instead. Pastel-hued watercolours, no larger than a paperback cover, of various

117

shells and, for a little added variety, starfish and seahorses too.

With the sunset, a chill quickly set in. There were open fires downstairs and a stack of logs, but the chimneys had been sealed in the upstairs rooms. Jack pulled on his thick Arran jumper and thought about climbing into bed. It wasn't that cold, but he felt ridiculously tired.

He carefully laid out Moira's *Ramones* t-shirt over the pillow on one side of the bed and finished the job he'd started the night before of unpacking her duffel. He didn't know quite what to expect, but unless he could find a use for black eyeliner, roll on deodorant, assorted t-shirts, jeans and ladies undies there wasn't much to help him.

As he'd expected, nestling at the bottom was her tape player and a collection of cassettes; *Ramones* (naturally), *Generation X, The Cramps, Skids, The Mekons, Sham 69, Black Flag, The Dead Kennedy's* (a personal favourite of Jack's). He'd once asked her what was wrong with Elton John?

Her reply hadn't been the kind of thing you could repeat to your mother. It had made Jack laugh though.

In the end, he settled for *The Clash*, which he found the least offensive of Moira's generally offensive music collection. He was pretty sure *The Clash* would be relieved to know that, and, after a moment's hiss, the furious slashing guitars of *Safe European Home* disturbed the quiet nooks and crannies of the House of Shells.

The Burrows-Things could wail all they liked, they were never going to out racket Moira's cassette collection.

Jack hooked his feet up onto the bed, cracked open his

one beer for the night, listened to Joe Strummer yell out of the little cassette player and eyed his selection of reading material. A story about a family snowed into an old haunted hotel or one about man-eating rats.

The perfect selection of books for a romantic getaway. Why hadn't he brought a comedy or a thriller? Nope, the haunted hotel or the man-eating rats. He thought of the gaping, flapping maws of the Burrows-Things and the ghostly woman fading into nothing before his eyes on Haunted Beach. Not to mention the lilting, playful laughter of the Giggle-finch and whatever he'd seen reflected in the TV.

Nope, he'd stick to beer and music for the time being.

*Last Gang in Town* finished and the house was returned to silence, Jack's beer can was starting to feel troublingly light. Would two beers be entirely unreasonable, given the situation?

In the distance, he heard the cackling wail of a Burrows-Thing, answered a moment later by another, the second sounded further away. Perhaps they were coming from far and wide for the party.

*There's loud music! There's cold beer! There's a little piggy for dinner!*

Jack fast forwarded the cassette and flipped it over to side two. Joe Strummer definitely sounded better than the Burrows-Things.

By the time Joe was swearing to tell nothing but the truth on *Guns on the Roof,* Jack had wandered through to the front bedroom. Like all good party hosts, he had a beer in one hand and a tyre iron in the other.

It was full dark; the moon was out and a protective cocoon

of light surrounded the House of Shells. Jack had left the curtains open in the front bedroom this time. You couldn't have too much light bleeding out into the night after all. Not when there were monsters about anyway.

He flicked off the light and crossed to the window, pulling back the nets for a better view. Things were moving out in the night again. Were there more of them now? It was hard to tell. He'd quite liked the fact they stuck to the shadows just beyond the reach of the patio lights, but tonight it felt strangely frustrating not quite knowing just how many of them were out there, let alone what they were.

Jack pinched his nose and sniffed his fingers, his eyes trying to see more than the night allowed. The Burrows-Things looked less tall and angular somehow, less, *inhuman*? Maybe it was just the angle of the moonlight (he'd heard it could be quite flattering at times) or was he just growing more familiar with them.

From the other bedroom, *The Clash* were singing about pissing on everyone in the classroom. He was positive Elton John had *never* sung about that.

Jack put the last of the beer where it could do the most good.

He placed the dead can on the window sill and sniffed his fingers again.

He'd been staring long enough for his eyes to adjust a little. Enough to make out the Burrows-Things a bit better anyway. There were three... no four, little knots of them, each gathered beneath the boughs of a tree. He could only really make them out when they moved, which they frequently did, swaying and moving and occasionally scurrying from one group to another. Jack thought of girls at a school disco, dancing together in little gangs and furtively hoping the boys were looking, now and then one of them hurrying over to another group to pass on the latest gossip about who fancied who.

Jack let the nets fall back and stepped backwards into the bedroom. As the only boy around he felt the image more than slightly unsettling.

Someone giggled in his ear.

Jack gave a cry and whirled around. The bedroom was deep in shadow, the only light was spilling in from the landing. Even so, he couldn't see anyone.

He swallowed and hurried over to the door, flicking the light switch back on. The room was empty.

"So, you want to talk now, huh?"

Whatever it was it didn't seem to mean him any harm. And what were a few disembodied giggles anyway? Unless he was going mad of course. Which was entirely possible.

"The beer's all gone I'm afraid. Not much of a party going on here..."

There was no reply other than Joe Strummer giving it some more.

"I guess all the real fun folk are outside..."

He was about to hurry back to the White Room when he noticed the wardrobe door was slightly ajar. Had it been like that before? He wasn't sure... but he didn't think so.

The wardrobe had been empty when he'd looked before and he didn't expect it to be any different now, but he pulled the door back anyway, just in case a giggling young woman had taken to hiding in there since the last time he looked.

121

There wasn't. Moira's leather jacket, however, was.

Jack blinked and stared at it in much the same way as if he'd found a unicorn munching a carrot amongst the mothballs and wire hangers.

Tentatively he reached out and run a hand along the cracked leather of the sleeve. It was definitely Moira's, she never wore anything else come rain or shine. She loved the tatty old thing that was probably older than she was. Weather-beaten and much abused with a red silk lining that had long since faded to a bemused pink.

"How, the fuck..."

Elsewhere in the House of Shells, someone giggled.

*

Either Moira had returned to the cottage and hung her jacket up or the Giggle-finch had spirited it away from The Burrows.

Jack sat on the edge of the bed in the White Room swinging his empty beer back and forth.

Of all the unlikely things he'd experienced since he'd arrived at the House of Shells, Moira returning to hang up her jacket seemed the most way out and ridiculous. She'd always been more of a throwing clothes over the nearest piece of furniture kind of girl.

Jack shook his head and flexed the sides of the empty can.

But if she had, then it meant she was alive.

The Burrows-Things hadn't eaten her. She was alive. Maybe.

Or the Giggle-finch had brought it back.

The idea some giggling, disembodied, house-tidying *thing* provided the more plausible explanation didn't hold out much hope for it being a sign Moira was still alive.

Jack crushed the can and tossed it aside.

He closed his eyes and listened to *The Clash* wail some more, pressing his fingers against his nose and breathing deeply.

He had to clear his head. He didn't know if Moira was alive or not, he didn't know what the Burrows-Things were, who the lady on the beach was, why the lane always brought him back to the House of Shells or what the fuck the Giggle-finch was.

But he knew tomorrow was another day and he needed to be up at dawn so he'd have every hour of daylight available to use to get away from the House of Shells. There had to be a way and having a clear head and a good night's sleep would help him figure it out.

He opened his eyes and stared at the crushed beer can sitting forlorn and discarded on the bedroom floor as Joe Strummer carried on giving it more juice on Moira's little cassette player.

*Sod it, might as well have another one.*

He somehow doubted Joe Strummer was a one can a night kind of a guy, so why should he be?

After wiping his fingers under his nose, Jack strolled out onto the landing, moved the chair wedged under the handle and unbolted the upstairs door. As he swung open the door, he heard something that had been masked by *The Clash's* manic guitars. Something that made his heart jump into his throat.

123

The phone was ringing…

"Don't hang up!"

Jack flew down the stairs, leaping the last few and hitting the floorboards with enough force to set the shell-laden shelves rocking as he half stumbled across to the small side table the phone sat on.

"Hello!" He shouted.

For a moment, the only response was the sound of breaking surf, then a woman's voice, faint but still audible above the waves.

"Hi, Jack, how you been keeping?"

It was Moira.

# Thirteen

Jack just stared at the cradle. There was no number written inside the dial, he noticed.

"Jack?"

"Moira... I thought you were dead."

"Don't be so silly."

"But you've been gone for days!"

"Sorry. Hard to explain. Call it family business, I had to go straight away. Summoned you might say. Kinda ruined our break, huh?"

"Well... it hasn't turned out quite how I'd hoped..."

Jack thought of long misshapen hands erupting from the sand.

"...not really."

"Promise I'll make it up to you. If you'll forgive me?"

Jack thought he should be bloody furious with her, but all he could feel was a relief so consuming he found he had slumped to the floor.

"Jack?"

"Yeah... fine..." he cleared his throat, which suddenly felt thick and hoarse "...just glad to hear from you. I've been so worried."

"I know... look I'm not going to get back for tomorrow. You ok going to London on your own. I'll catch up with you when

I get back. Guess I got some *serious* making up to do, huh?"

He should be furious. He really should. Everything that had happened over the last few days and nights. Everything he *thought* had happened too. Instead, all he wanted to do was hold her.

"A bit."

"Fair enough. I should be back in London in a couple of days-"

"Moira, sorry, there's a slight problem."

*Fuck, she's going to think I've gone mad.*

Cabin fever at least, or some strange brain infection from a funny sausage maybe.

"What kind of problem?" She asked, her voice becoming slow and precise. A gull was making a racket somewhere at her end.

"I can't get out."

"You're locked in the cottage?"

"No... look, this is going to sound crazy, but I'm stuck. Every time I go back down the lane the way we come in, I end up back here. I've tried walking out and I can't get off the beach, there's no way through the woods..."

"Oh..."

Jack could hear the edge of panic in his own voice. Or did he just sound plain deranged? He didn't think she'd believe him, though, frankly, he didn't care. Right now he'd settle for her calling an ambulance for him and being carted away in a straightjacket.

"And there are these *things* outside... at night..."

*This really doesn't sound good.*

"Fuck," was Moira's pithy response.

"I'm not making it up!" Jack groped for the right words to prove both his sincerity and sanity, "I've only had one beer!"

Moira was silent; there was nothing but the pounding of surf interrupted by the occasional gull's screech. A distant part of Jack's mind was wondering how he could hear the sea so clearly, but he ignored it, his mind should be worrying about other things at this precise moment. Like getting Moira to believe him.

"Moira?"

"Did you cross the circle?"

Jack blinked, "Sorry?"

"At the top of the largest dune, there's a wooden circle. Did you enter it at night?"

"Erm... yes..."

"Shit."

More gulls, more waves.

"Moira... these things... they, I know it sounds mad, but-"

"It's ok Jack, don't worry about them."

"You... *know* about them?"

"They're harmless Jack... Well, *pretty* harmless."

"*Pretty harmless?* Have you fucking seen them?!"

"Yeah, I have. Look, Jack, just stay indoors at night. They can't come into the house-"

"I figured that."

"Good. Whatever you do, don't go out at night."

"What happens if I go out at night?" Jack asked before he could stop himself.

"Just... stay indoors. Promise me Jack?"

"Sure. I'll stay in. I've got beer, I've got *The Clash*. No need to go out."

"Are you playing my cassettes?"

"There's not much on TV."

Moira giggled, "Well, at least, I've got you listening to decent music of your own free will. So it's not been a complete waste."

Jack would still have preferred Elton John, but he stopped himself mentioning the choices of beggars.

"Yeah. Wonders, eh? Hey, Moira, where *are* you? Paddling?"

A long sigh filled his ear, it reminded him a little of the noise she made in his ear as they clung to each other in the darkness after passions had finally been spent.

"I'll explain. Promise. I owe you that much. But not now, not enough time... I gotta go soon."

"Ok... I don't really care about anything else. I'm just glad you're... ok," Jack swallowed, "I love you M."

Gulls and waves then, in a small distant voice, "Do you, really?"

Yeah, he realised, he did.

"Have to go, Jack," she said, before he could reply, "all that matters is that you stay inside."

"Moira, nothing on Earth is going to get me out of this house."

"Then you'll be ok..." she said, her voice just a kiss above the surf. Then she was gone.

"Bye love..." Jack whispered.

He was shaking too much to put the handset back, so he held it against his face for a minute or two as if it kept him closer to Moira. A couple of choking sobs racked his chest and he screwed up his eyes against the unexpected tears.

Eventually, he reached up from the floor where he was still sprawled to put the handset back but froze before he could find the cradle.

He was looking behind the table at the wire hanging from the phone, hanging all the way down to where it was cut.

The phone wasn't connected to anything.

# Fourteen

Jack didn't sleep so well that night.

His mind was still spinning too much from his phone call with Moira. The fact she was alive, that she seemed to know something about what was going on, that the phone wasn't connected to anything, plus the Burrows-Things incessant wailing, cackling, bawling and howling, all combined to keep sleep at bay.

But the thing, perversely, keeping him awake the most, other than the four beers he'd eventually sunk, was that he'd told Moira he loved her.

*Do you, really?*

Had he meant it? Had it just been relief she was alive? Had it simply been because it was the thing you were expected to say?

He'd gone out of his way not to utter those little words over the three months he'd been seeing Moira. He knew he was infatuated and intoxicated by her. Who wouldn't be? She was beautiful. And smart, and funny and kind-hearted and sexy as hell. There was nothing bad he could say about her, save possibly her dubious taste in music.

And maybe the fact she was pretty much half his age.

As the Burrows-Things had howled at the moon (or each other, or a passing rabbit, he was passed caring), he tried to drag his thoughts back to more immediate concerns.

Like what the hell was going on?

But his mind proved to be a treacherous friend that kept stealing back to think about Moira. It was as if he'd walled off all thoughts of her when he'd believed her dead, but now that wall had broken and everything was rushing out. Including stuff he hadn't known had been there in the first place.

*Do you, really?*

Eventually, he'd turned the light off in the hope it would help him sleep. It was strange how much more sinister and unsettling deformed, unnatural, creatures of the night sounded in the darkness.

Who would have thought?

Jack was sure he should be angry. She'd run off and left him, let him think her dead when all she had to do was call him on the (totally not connected) phone and tell him everything was ok. She was alive. The monsters from The Burrows weren't going to eat him. Well, at least as long as he didn't go outside at night.

But it wouldn't come. Instead, he laid Moira's t-shirt over the pillow and hugged it. He wasn't entirely sure if that was the sort of thing a grown man should be doing, but, hell. Who was going to tell?

He needed to go home tomorrow. Amanda would call, expecting him to be there so he could bore her senseless with anecdotes from the imaginary *Designing the Future* conference. But he didn't want to go. He didn't want to go back to that life. He wanted to be here, with Moira, monsters or not.

But there was no guarantee when Moira would be back from whatever the hell had kept her away. What had she said? Family business? He knew nothing about her family. He'd asked, of course, but she'd been vague and evasive. He assumed there was bad blood or bad memories. Something she didn't want to talk about anyway, so he hadn't pressed her about it. Now he thought maybe he should have.

Well, going home wasn't an issue for now, he couldn't. He was trapped. All he could hope for was that Moira knew a way out. She knew about the Burrows-Things, so maybe that wasn't such a forlorn hope.

At some point, he drifted off into restless dreams where he was being chased across the beach. The faster he ran, the deeper his feet sunk into the sand until he was knee deep in it, ploughing through like a man trying to run on powdered snow; all the time hearing the panting, jabbering sound of his pursuers, but unable to look over his shoulders to see them.

He awoke with a start and a strangled gasp. Disorientated not by the lingering coils of his dream, but by the fact he was standing at the window, stark naked, fingers pushed hard against his nostrils, filling them with a dry musky scent that was very much not Moira.

He jerked his hand away and jumped back from the window.

"What the fuck..."

He'd never sleepwalked in his life, but not only had he gotten out of bed, but he'd also gone through to the front bedroom.

A sound came out of the night, not the Burrows-Things,

but women's laughter. At first, he thought it was the Gigglefinch again, but the laughter was deeper and throatier. Somehow more *knowing*. And it was coming from outside the House of Shells.

He stepped back towards the window and pressed his nose against the glass. Without even realising he was doing it, he fumbled with the catch and pushed the window up in stiff irregular increments.

The night air rushed in; cool on his skin and scented with a dry, fleshy aroma that made him want to suck it deeply into his lungs. Things were moving in the trees, but different to the awkward, ungainly scurrying figures he'd seen before, these were lithe, smooth forms filled with grace and vitality.

It took him a moment before he realised his cock was stiffening.

"Jesus!"

The window suddenly slammed down and he jumped backwards, his hands instinctively cupping his manhood despite not being *that* close to the window.

The window was old and the catch was clearly loose. However, when he tried to force the window open again (without really knowing why) he found it'd frozen into place and wouldn't budge.

He felt a twist of annoyance as part of him wanted to lean out of the window into the chill, still night and drink that scent. He had a pretty fair idea which part of him too.

Jack snapped the curtains shut and hurried back through to the White Room, jumping into bed he slid under the covers and pulled the sheets up to his chin. His hand flailed in the darkness till he found the soft, worn cotton of Moira's t-shirt which he pressed against his face. His heart was racing, hard, urgent thumps that hurt his chest. God, was he having a heart attack?

He breathed deeply through the t-shirt till all he could smell was the sweet lingering fragrance of Moira's perfume. It smelt like sanity.

Jack hunkered down and stared into the darkness. Still clutching Moira's t-shirt, he waited for the dawn.

\*

Mist had rolled in from the sea, masking the sunrise and diffusing the morning. The trees were just ghosts dissolving into the greyness, the dunes entirely concealed beyond.

Jack was back in the front bedroom though this time it had been a conscious decision to leave his bed and stare out of the window. At least partly anyway.

His fingers rested on the window lock. He'd intended to open it to let some fresh air in but had hesitated, knowing that wasn't true. The air in the house was fresh enough and he could feel the chill autumn morning through the glass. He wanted to know if that scent lingered in the mist.

*Why?*

It was the stink of monsters.

Something raw and primal, something unnatural and wrong, yet he felt drawn to it, intoxicated by it. He craved it. He thought of those things, those horrible, awful things erupting out of the sand. Those nightmarish figures jerking towards him in the blinking orange flash of the hazard light.

But it wasn't enough. Besides, he needed to unjam the window in case he -

Jack undid the catch and found the window slid smoothly upwards. Whatever had snagged it in the night must have worked its way free.

The air was cold enough to make him gasp. He was naked and his skin tingled with the morning's touch. It didn't stop him leaning out of the window and drinking down enough air to make him shudder though

It smelt of damp wood and mulching leaves, tinged with the faint briny hint of the sea. Nothing else.

He peered into the mist, wondering if it was still monster's playtime, the mist offering enough of a cloak against the sun to stop them scurrying back to wherever they spent the daylight hours. Beneath the fine dry sands of the dune field he supposed.

Nothing moved. Not even a bird. No gulls cried, no branches stirred, even the sea had fallen silent without the wind to whip up any surf. No figures were hidden in the grey, no cackling cries, no maddening howls. Nothing but his heart could be heard, no movement but the steam of his breath.

The mist had covered the world and stripped it of all colour, sound and movement.

For the first time since Moira had run off into The Burrows, Jack felt like he might be the only man left alive in the whole world.

He brought the window down; the sound of it slamming seemed loud enough to shake the House of Shells to its foundations.

Despite shivering Jack stood for a few minutes, staring out into the grey world, nothing approaching a thought in his head, just a damp insistent clawing somewhere behind his eyes. A combination of a hangover and a bad night's sleep. Deep down, however, he knew it was something else entirely.

Eventually, he yanked his gaze away from the window. He tried to find something else to capture his mind. The room didn't offer much save for a collection of conch shells lining the mantle, a treasure from a warmer more exotic sea than the flat and unnaturally silent one beyond the dunes.

He let his fingers brush one. It was cream, broken with ridges of brown, inside the valve it was as smooth as glass and flushed to a bright pink. He slipped his fingers inside it and smiled despite himself at what it reminded him of. Jack made to lift it to his ear to listen to the sea. Then remembered the sound of the waves he'd heard on the phone downstairs and left it alone.

Other than the obligatory drawings of shells, a couple of old black and white photographs hung on the wall, the kind your Great Aunt might decorate her sideboard with as memorials to a distant youth.

One was a studio portrait of a good-looking young man, razor-starched collars rising from beneath a dark buttoned jacket. With his hair loosely swept back and his arms folded, he stared glassily off camera, nothing that passed for an expression on his well-proportioned face. Jack suspected he had quite a smile on him, the kind that would probably have made those proper Victorian ladies blush if he'd known how to use it.

The second photograph was of a raven-haired young woman paddling in the sea in one of those old-fashioned bathing costumes that left everything to the imagination; a dark dress, with a high waist that flared as it fell to her thighs, with sailor's collars and a (presumably) white trim. Beneath the dress she wore knee-length leggings that were about as racy as a respectable woman was probably allowed to get away with in those days. She wore a straw boater, one clearly too big for her, which she was touching with her right hand as she bent slightly forward, a bright, infectious smile dimpling her face as she looked at the camera. No serious posing here. The photograph was time-faded and sepia-tinged; a single moment that had survived from an otherwise long forgotten day.

Jack stared at the photograph for a long time and wondered why he hadn't looked at it before.

The girl in the picture was Moira.

# Fifteen

Dawn came on slow as winter that morning, its murky light reluctantly revealing the shroud of mist which had been laid upon the world. The fallen leaves beneath Jack's feet were soggy with dew. The trees stood about him, silent and brooding. Unmoving ghosts. No birds sang, no gulls cried. The mist was as thick as bathroom steam, eddying about him in sheets of twisting, restless moisture.

Without really thinking about what he was doing he'd dressed and come outside in the first muted light of the day to bask in the pungent scent of monsters.

He'd found a spot where their scent was strongest and it had rooted him as firmly as the surrounding trees. His breath came in short, harsh pants. His heart was thumping hard again. He felt light-headed almost to the point of giddiness. The most disturbing thing, however, was his arousal which was insistent and almost painful.

He well remembered being a sexually repressed teenager, when even the most furtive glance at a pretty girl had been enough to send the blood in his body rushing south like water down a plughole.

This was worse.

Unconsciously he had started to vigorously rub his erection.

*What the hell is wrong with me?*

He snatched his hand away and clasped it tightly with the other as if it no longer formed part of his body. It trembled in his grip.

With slow, deliberate steps, he backed away from the trees. The scent wrapped itself around his flesh, gently tugging and teasing, as reluctant to let him leave as a lover from a crumpled bed. Or a fly from a spider's web.

A small guttural cry wrenched itself from his throat as he spun away to sprint through the mist. The spectral forms of trees slipped by in soft grey blurs till his feet were slapping the uneven planks of the boardwalk, half submerged in sand.

The dunes rose either side of him, the tops lost in the dour, foreboding mist. He slowed to a walking pace but didn't stop. He could still smell them, albeit more faintly, and he was pretty sure what he could still smell was on his own skin.

The beach was eerily silent and painted in shifting bands of grey. He couldn't even see the sea let alone hear it. The sand, clean, unbroken and moistened by the mist, stretched maybe twenty paces before it disappeared completely into the murk.

He kept walking, head down, hands in pockets, till the ocean, differentiated only by being a darker tinted grey than the rest of the world, slowly emerged. A few derisory ripples were all that moved as the sea breathed up and down the beach. It was impossible to see where the water ended and the sky began; the edges of the world were just grey formless smears.

He stood and listened to the silent sea. The waves were no more than a lover's breath in the darkness. Further down the beach, Jack could just make out a few ever-hungry gulls roaming the shoreline and occasionally pecking at the sand, but even they seemed to have been muted by the mist.

Jack kicked off his boots. Even in his coat he was cold, but he shrugged that off too and ignored the shivers as he stripped to his underpants, then peeled them off as well. He was sure the sight didn't bother the gulls much, even though he felt like some almighty variety of pervert standing butt naked and shivering on the sand behind a fearsome erection.

He bundled his clothes together and waded in without pause.

The water was shockingly cold. A million tiny needles tormented his flesh, but he splashed onwards until the sea was above his waist, then dived under and begun to swim. His breath tried to explode out of him. How much colder could the sea get before ice formed on it?

He swam out as far as he dared; laboured gasping and the splash of his thrashing arms the only sounds on the flat grey water. His body warmed with the exertion and acclimatised to the ambient water temperature. Or he was simply so numb he was no longer capable of feeling anything much. When he did stop, his feet couldn't find the bottom. He trod water, his ragged breath adding to the mist draped over the sea. He couldn't make out the shore; the ocean bled seamlessly into the fallen sky. The world was empty.

A blank, grey page upon which nothing had yet been drawn.

Jack let the cold empty his mind and the saltwater

scour his skin. The rhythm of his body as it trod water his only concern. He could smell nothing but the brine of the sea. The icy water had done wonders for his unwanted hard-on too.

He may have been there for a few minutes, maybe longer. Probably longer. He drifted for a while.

*Is this how people drown?*

Not in a whirl of arms, flailing legs and choking screams, but a slow, peaceful acceptance of something so much greater and more powerful than yourself. The realisation you are nought but another tiny speck of flesh in an endless and eternal sea of life.

Spluttering, he spat out seawater, his limbs suddenly leaden and stiff. He'd been out here too long.

He was about to strike for shore when something moved on the water. His head snapped around, convinced he'd seen something out of the corner of his eye. Ripples were spreading out on the grey water. Something had been there.

Just a fish. A big fish maybe. He remembered the giant severed head he'd stumbled across on the beach and became instantly conscious of himself dangling enticingly in the water. He started swimming as urgently as his limbs would allow.

Something moved beneath him.

The water was too dark to see anything, but he'd felt *something*. Not directly touching his skin, but the pressure of water displaced by it moving below him. Something moving much faster. Something pretty big too.

Big enough to bite a giant fish's head clean off?

The thought that he was just a speck of flesh on the sea

141

came again...

He tried swimming faster, though he suspected he was simply splashing more and going nowhere any quicker. The salt water stung his eyes and he tried peering for sight of the land between flailing strokes, but everything was still endless soft grey save for the water he was frothing up around him.

Forcing himself to calm down and stop, he tried to touch bottom but there was still nothing beneath him. Nothing he wanted to put his feet on anyway. Surely he hadn't swum very far out. Had he? The realisation dawned that just because the sea was a flat grey sheet, it didn't mean a current wasn't imperceptibly pulling him away from the beach.

Out to where the really big fish swam.

*Shit.*

Jack took a couple of shuddering breaths before starting to swim again. This time, he stuck to breaststroke so he could, at least, see ahead of him. The sea was still flat calm and he swam for a couple more minutes without any hint of the shoreline emerging out of the mist.

He was about to stop again and see if his feet could find bottom when a shape rose out of the water before him. Jack came to a spluttering halt, managing to gulp a mouthful of the ocean before his tiring arms and legs were able to tread enough water to keep his mouth above the sea.

At first, he thought another swimmer had emerged from the water, but as he blinked away seawater from his eyes he realised whatever it was, it wasn't human.

Though it had the torso of a man, its skin was a mottled silver-grey, hairless and translucent enough for Jack to be able to make out the faint network of pulsing blue veins beneath. The figure's head was also hairless, and the jaw and flattened nose protruded into something vaguely resembling a snout, with two flaring slits for nostrils. The eyes were large and completely black as far as Jack could tell. The figure was utterly still in the water as if standing on the bottom rather than treading water. His own feet were still not finding sand.

A hand emerged from the sea and the creature pointed at Jack. A thin membrane of flesh connected each of its five fingers.

Jack stared at it. Unsure what it meant. It didn't seem to want to eat him at least.

The creature's finger jabbed forward again.

Jack tentatively poked at his chest and managed to keep his mouth above water just long enough to croak, "Jack... me Jack."

The creature blinked its large, liquid eyes and let out a stream of clicks and shrieks. Was it laughing?

Once its merriment had subsided it tried pointing again, this time lifting its arm above its head and making more vigorous pointing motions. Jack just looked on blankly.

The creature's nostrils flared a couple of times and it dived back under the water. There was a glimpse of a large silver tail and then it was gone.

A mermaid? An actual fucking *mermaid!*

He looked wildly around to see where it had gone.

The creature appeared to be male, so he supposed merman might be more accurate. It seemed the monsters didn't just come out at night here after all.

He was just thinking it had gone when the merman rose out of the water about twenty feet behind him. This time, he lifted his hand and made a gesture Jack understood well enough.

*Come with me.*

But that was further out to sea.

Weren't mermaids supposed to lure sailors to their deaths? That was how the old folk tale went. But what about mermen, did they have the same hobby?

Jack shook his head and pointed the other way, "The beach, I have to swim to the beach!"

The merman shook his own head in return, sending droplets splattering over the motionless sea. He let out another series of screeches and clicks. These ones didn't sound like laughter. More like agitation.

The mist was still obscuring the world. Was it possible he'd become disorientated and swam further out to sea? It was entirely possible. And now a merman had popped out of the water to give him directions. On a normal day...

Jack tried swimming a few strokes away from the creature. When he stopped and looked back, it had slipped beneath the water again. His legs and arms were going numb, whether from the cold or the unaccustomed strain of actually having to do something. He wasn't sure which, but neither was good. He needed to get to the beach and quickly. But did he trust his own judgement or that of... a fish?

Of course, the creature might not have meant anything. It might be no smarter than a seal or a salmon and was just being playful.

The merman erupted out of the water just in front of

him and started gesticulating agitatedly, stabbing its webbed finger over Jack's shoulder. The merman was close enough for Jack to know it ate a lot of raw fish.

Tiny flecks of silver swirled in its large black eyes. The face, even with its slightly protruding snout and slits for nostrils carried a human resemblance, but those big, black eyes were entirely alien. Still, Jack sensed no malice in them.

"Ok... let's try... your way..."

He turned and tried swimming in the other direction. The clicks and shrieks of the merman immediately ceased and the creature fell alongside him in the water. It kept pace with the same ease Jack could match the stride of a geriatric lady in a zimmer frame.

"Don't suppose you know a way out of here, huh?" he managed to ask between pitiful breaststrokes.

The merman made a whistling noise that Jack took to sound apologetic.

"Pity."

He wasn't sure how long he should keep going. He could easily be swimming ever further out to sea. The merman's strange dark eyes were fixed upon him as he swam effortlessly alongside. Jack thought he could only see curiosity it the creature's eyes and expressions, but then he was the first to admit, even after fifteen years of marriage, he sometimes still had trouble knowing when Amanda was pissed with him. It often took some inventively fruity language before the penny finally dropped.

"You sure the beach is this way?"

Two clicks and a kind of cat-being-sick coughing noise. And a sharp movement of head up and down. Was that a nod?

"Can... you... understand... me?" Apart from the shivering gasps, he asked the question in much the same way he would to a Spanish waiter.

The merman moved effortlessly forward, racing through the water at incredible speed before disappearing into the mist and leaving only the faintest of ripples in its wake.

He didn't know whether to take that as a yes or a no and was still trying to convince himself he should turn around when the beach gradually materialised beyond the still water. His feet found silken sand and he emerged, panting and shivering.

"Thank you!" He managed to shout into the mist. A click and some whistles came back out of the murk, followed by a splash. Then the world was silent again.

Staggering through the shallows and back onto the beach, seawater fell like rain from his body.

He bent half forward, hands on knees, and let out a few more shivering gasps. He was still ankle deep in water as the sea rippled back and forth around him.

He could see no sign of his clothes. The current must have taken him along the beach. But which way?

Jack tried left. Despite his exhaustion, he managed to jog along the water's edge, by now far too cold to feel absurd. Thankfully, it took only a few minutes to find his clothes. If he'd thought this through, he would have brought a towel. Instead, he just pulled his clothes over his wet skin before shuffling above the tide line, where he hunkered down on the dry sand, huddling inside his coat and fiercely hugging his knees to stop himself shaking.

He felt better. Cold, wet, miserable and probably well on his way to getting pneumonia, but better. He could no longer detect the musky scent of monsters on his skin. And his cock had shrivelled pretty much all the way into his pelvis. Possibly permanently. But at least he'd made a new friend.

"What the fuck is this place..."

Pulling himself to his feet he trudged back towards the House of Shells, damp clothes fusing to his sand-caked, shiver-raked skin.

It occurred to him as he shuffled through the sand that a cold shower might have been a helluva lot easier.

\*

The mist hung around for most of the day, eventually fading to a distant haze beneath the leaden clouds, but never entirely vanishing.

After standing under the hot shower until he could feel his fingers and toes again, he cooked breakfast, finishing the last of the bacon and the baked beans in the process. He barely registered the fact the dirty cutlery, plate and pans from the previous night had been washed and stacked up on the drainer again. Burrows-Things, giant glowing butterflies, mermen... What was a kitchen that did its own washing up?

Later he mooched around the cottage, not entirely sure what to do with himself or his aching limbs. He spent a fair amount of time staring at the phone, and twice checked to make sure the cable really was cut. He picked it up once and heard the same distant roar of the surf. Tentatively he'd called Moira's name. There was no reply.

He went upstairs to stare at the old photograph on the

147

bedroom wall with the girl that looked so much like Moira. It obviously wasn't Moira, it just *looked* like her. A relative? Her grandmother maybe? She was local after all and the fact that the House of Shells was connected to her family was just one of a long list of things she'd overlooked mentioning to him.

Alternatively, it was a modern photograph of Moira done in an old-fashioned style, like the pictures you could get at seaside resorts where they dressed you up in period clothes. It certainly *looked* old. Faded and scratched, but he supposed it could be faked to look like that. Both sounded like entirely logical explanations to Jack.

There was probably a logical explanation as to how she could call him on a phone that wasn't connected, meeting a merman and for things that burst out of the sand too.

Though none came immediately to mind.

Jack tried to distract himself by flicking through the building specs he'd brought along to impress Moira. On reflection, why he'd thought she'd be impressed with plans for a multi-storey car park in Milton Keynes now escaped him utterly.

*I've spent my life designing shit like this...*

Car parks, shopping malls, tower blocks; drab concrete abominations to blight the landscape. Hadn't he wanted to design beautiful buildings once? Things people would admire and love and remember. He looked again at the concrete box he was going to help dump onto the world. It was functional and even possibly useful, but as ugly as a sun-dried dog turd and just as likely to draw admiring glances.

After huddling on the sofa with the paperwork spread across his lap and watching his breath steam, his eye fell on the basket of logs by the fire. No reason not to be warm.

It turned out fire lighting was something else he could add to the long and distinguished list of things he was rubbish at. It took the best part of an hour to get the logs burning properly. A journey that took him through irritation, frustration, creative language, a couple of slightly singed fingers and a stiff back until he finally arrived at a fuzzy sense of achievement as the hitherto stubbornly incombustible wood finally bent to the will of man and began to crackle, pop and fill the House of Shells with the aroma of wood smoke.

Crouched in front of the fire, he slowly tore up the building specs before crunching each page into a tight ball and tossing it onto the fire. Each one flared briefly before crumpling into charred flakes within the greater fire. As each one disappeared, Jack felt strangely liberated. The next six months of his working life was more or less scheduled to be consumed by that project. It was a headache he didn't even realise he was suffering from till he'd gotten rid of it. Let someone else help deface the world, he'd done his share.

He celebrated by stretching out on the sofa to admire the pirouetting twists of flame. He'd then promptly fallen asleep.

By the time he woke up the fire had burned itself out.

After glaring blearily at the embers, he swore and decided to go for a drive.

It was never going to be a long drive, but he trundled up and down the lane, or, more accurately, down and further down, a few times just for the hell of it.

The car smelt of a world he understood, where things

behaved to a set order of agreed rules, a world of metal and petrol, vinyl, plastic and imitation wood. He even remembered there was an old John Denver cassette in the glove compartment that Moira had banned him, on pain of things unmentionable, from ever playing in her presence.

He stuck the cassette in as he bumped along the lane in anticipation of listening to music that had a tune and words he could sing along to. He didn't know whether to laugh or cry when *Take Me Home, Country Roads* filled the Cortina.

He settled for taking it as one more sign that the world hated him.

*

Despite Moira's assertion she wouldn't be back that day, Jack kept expecting her to come bursting through the door at any moment to rescue him. Possibly on a white charger. Well, a pony at least.

By the time the gloom began thickening to dusk, he'd stopped looking out of the window for white horses and pretty girls and turned his attention to whipping up another of his delicious pasta concoctions of mushroom, onion, tomato and cheese. He was thinking of christening it a cheesy tomato onion and mushroom pasta supreme. That or pasta slop. It was no surprise to find his breakfast mess had been tidied up while he'd been out.

*Pixies, fairies or Julie Andrews?*

"Thanks!" He'd cheerily called out, but no response came, giggly or otherwise.

He ate in the kitchen, suffering each mouthful while being serenaded by a lucky dip selection from Moira's bag of shouty three-chord music. The winner had been *The Slits*, who were a breath of fresh air compared to most of Moira's bands, insomuch as they had a girl shouting incoherently into a microphone, rather than a guy.

At least, they hadn't done a cover of *Take Me Home, Country Roads.*

By the time the remnants of his meal had been consigned to the bin, the dark was pressing in at the windows. After dumping the plate and pans in the sink to be magically washed up, he lit the House of Shells and decided to put his last three cans of beer to work. His one a night strategy had been blown out of the water the previous evening, so, he might as well get the job finished.

He used his trusty tyre iron to poke the embers in the fireplace about. There was no fireguard and he wanted to make sure he didn't burn the cottage down during the night. Once satisfied the fire was well and truly dead he straightened up, glancing at the TV screen as he did so.

A girl was standing behind him in the reflection.

He span around but the room was as empty as his every other sense told him it was.

Part of Jack didn't want to look back at the TV. Better to take his beers, go upstairs and tell himself he hadn't seen anything reflected in the screen but distorted shadows. Just like last time.

Instead, he backed across the room, tyre iron still in his hand just on the off chance it might be useful in dealing with a ghostly reflected apparition. Crouching down by the side of the TV, he twisted around and stared into the dark reflection within the curved glass, ignoring his own fairground mirror likeness he expected nothing else to be there. You only ever glimpsed ghosts out of the corner of your eye, didn't you? The bogeyman was never there when you looked twice.

That might be true for the bogeyman, but it clearly wasn't for the invisible girl he shared the House of Shells with.

She was standing behind the sofa, head slightly lowered so her long dark hair fell about her face. Between the hair and the distorted reflection, he couldn't really make out her features, though he saw enough to know she was staring intently at him.

When he'd glimpsed her before he'd thought she was wrapped in rags, but, he now realised, she was actually draped in tendrils of smoke, shifting and coiling about her, translucent, restless snakes of steam.

"Who are you?" Jack saw his lips move in the dark glass.

The girl covered her mouth with a bony hand and a faint, coy giggle floated across the room, though it seemed to be coming from much further away than the other side of the sofa.

"You helped me, the other night, to get away from the Burrows-Things, didn't you?"

The girl in the TV nodded.

"Thank you."

There was the hint of a shrug. With her face permanently lowered she could have been any surly monosyllabic teenager. Apart from the curls of smoke around her pale skin and the fact he could only see her reflection of course.

152

There were a thousand things he wanted to ask the girl, even if the only answer he would ever get would be a disembodied giggle, but before he could say anything more, she turned and went up the stairs.

"Thanks for the washing up too!" he called after her, turning to look at the stairs, which were pointedly devoid of apparitions.

He still heard her giggle though.

*

Once the downstairs was lit and secured, he retreated up to the White Room to fritter away another night with music he didn't want to listen to and books he didn't want to read. The beer he had no issue with.

There was no sign of the girl upstairs, other than the neatly made bed. It struck him there were no mirrors in the House of Shells; the only reflections to be found were the dark, distorted ones in the dead TV screen in the living room. Where the Giggle-finch lived.

He supposed she was here, standing at the edge of the bed watching him. Despite the fact he didn't think she meant him any harm and seemed intent only in ensuring the cottage didn't descend into complete squalor during his stay, the thought made him feel both uncomfortable and vulnerable.

Invisible friends were all well and good, but when they turned out to be real...

Jack sat Moira's cassette player on his lap and filled the bedroom with shouty, foul-mouthed music which was, at least, effective in being louder than the Burrows-Things as he sipped beer and stared at the ceiling. Moira's t-shirt was next to him and he fingered it absent-mindedly as he drank. He thought about getting the photo from the front bedroom but decided against it. He didn't know if there was a name for staring longingly at pictures of your lover's grandmother, but it sounded distinctly unhealthy.

By the time he'd finished the second can he was humming along to *Black Flag* and Jack fell asleep before he'd finished the third. *The Buzzcocks* providing the lullaby. By the time the tape hissed into silence, and the Burrows-Things had started singing, he was snoring soundly.

Fingers lightly pressing against his nostrils.

# Sixteen

Jack sat up and climbed out of bed, the sheets spilling onto the floor after him. He stood for a few seconds, head tilted slightly to one side. The house was silent, but beyond, out in the night, a song was being sung. The same one over and over as it had been for hours. Calling him softly.

His eyes moved, though his lids remained closed and his mouth hung agape. His breath was a wet and thick snore. He moved across the room with the jerky, hesitant steps of a marionette, only coming to a halt when the bedroom door slammed shut in his face.

Slowly he reached out and curled his fingers around the handle and pulled at the door. At first, it wouldn't budge and he had to yank it hard several times to overcome whatever was pulling it shut from the other side.

The lights on the landing were flashing on and off, but as his eyes were still closed that didn't register and he moved down the stairs regardless. The TV burst into life as he reached the bottom of the stairs, a roaring hiss of white noise from the static-filled screen.

It made no difference to Jack as he shuffled towards the front door, nor did he feel the cushions that flew across the room to bounce off him or the telephone that rung loud enough to rattle the table it sat on as he passed it.

The front door was as reluctant to open as the bedroom one had been, but he was strong enough to eventually force it open and walk out into the night. The song grew louder as he crossed the threshold and down the garden path towards it.

As he moved on to the lane, a lump of rock dislodged from the garden wall and dropped onto his foot hard enough for him to cry out and his eyes sprung open.

*

Whatever he'd stubbed his toes on he'd done it hard enough to make him cry out and stumble. For a moment he stood, disorientated, trying to focus on the darkness and work out why his foot hurt, why he was so cold and why he wasn't still in bed.

And furthermore, why had he left the House of Shells?

He was still in the pool of radiance thrown out by the cottage's lights, but only just. He was in the lane, his bare feet already wet from the damp mulch of leaves carpeting the ground. The shadows of trees and gorse were scattered before him, spectral in the soft glow of the mist which had crept back with the setting sun, not as thick as it had been during the day, but enough to blur the edges of the night.

And in the mist figures stood waiting.

Then he heard the singing. Not the cackling, jabbering howls of the Burrows-Things, but something musical, a whisper of song on the air, high, haunting and gentle, an undulating melody sung by many voices spread out around him so the song surrounded and caressed him as much as the tendrils of mist did.

156

There was another sound too. Coming from the house. A distant, tittering sound. The Giggle-finch? But different, more a nervous, frightened snicker than the usual playful giggle. Part of him thought he should look back at the cottage, but the sound was so distant and unimportant compared to the song. It was too much effort. What would he see anyway? There were no reflections out here for that slender, dark-haired girl to live in.

Jack found his feet were moving him forward. The voices, beautiful and ethereal in the mist-softened darkness, compelling him to come closer so he might hear them better.

He didn't understand the words being sung, they were in no language he recognised, but he knew it was a song of love and hope and joy all the same. The song grew in pitch as he neared the figures. He still couldn't see them entirely clearly, but they weren't Burrows-Things. A line of young women stood before him, tall, lithe and pale. Wrapped in twists of cloth as translucent as the mist, hair hanging long and wild to their breasts; beautiful women...

*Just... stay indoors. Promise me Jack?*

He'd promised Moira, hadn't he? The memory seemed somewhat fuzzy. Thinking about it, had he actually talked to Moira at all? The phone wasn't connected, so he supposed he couldn't have. It must have been a dream. That made sense.

The mist and the singing enveloped him along with a scent; sweet, pungent, demanding, it perfumed the chill air with desire and lust. It grew stronger as the women gathered around him, still singing their strange lilting high-pitched song. Their words crept into his mind, dampening and diffusing his thoughts the way the mist softened the outlines

157

of the trees.

He could see them now, all about him. Even with the darkness and the mist he could tell they were all stunningly beautiful, their full-lipped mouths teasing, turning and coiling around each unearthly word they sang.

They were reaching out, their long, long, slender fingers caressing his skin; dry, smooth and warm their touch drove out the night's bitter air and fired his soul as well as his body

He wanted them. All of them.

Big eyes watched him, sparkling darkly in the night; liquid, darting, both coy and bold. Mischievous, playfully knowing eyes. Eyes full of promises.

One moved to stand in front of him, her voice, reverberating through his bones, was like the sweet sing-song call of an exotic tropical bird. Her hair, which fell, in long spiralling twists, nearly to her waist, was the colour of sand on a summer beach.

*...all that matters is that you stay inside.*

Moira again.

Hadn't he loved her once? He couldn't remember. It didn't matter, nothing mattered but the song and the singers leading him out of the scattered trees towards The Burrows. He was pretty sure he loved them now.

The song weaving about him was interspersed with throaty, flirtatious laughter. A dark-haired beauty with skin like talc save for the petal-blush of her cheeks, examined him with eyes the colour of burnt honey as she took his hand, sending a thrill of anticipation jolting up his arm. She was slowly rolling her fat bottom lip back and forth between her teeth.

*...nothing on Earth is going to get me out of this house...*

That hadn't been Moira. That had been him. Not the first time he'd been wrong about something. No way. But he thought this was going to be worth being wrong about.

Other hands were on him as his feet pushed into the soft sand of the dunes. He was wearing pyjama bottoms and a faded grey t-shirt and their insistent hands were pushing beneath to stroke his skin. He gasped as a hand momentarily gripped his hardness. Other sounds broke the rhythm of their song; panted, guttural sounds of longing and need. Some of them may well have been his own.

They were pressing about him on all sides, half lifting him with the pressure of their bodies so his feet only seemed to be grazing the sand. His own hands were reaching about him, feeling their bodies where they were soft and where they were firm.

Lips grazed his in a flash of molten flowing hair. Her kiss tasted both sweet and bitter, like sugared seawater, but it was only a fleeting moment before another set of lips were on his and he felt a tongue pushing into his mouth.

Laughter and song and the distant hum of the ocean, the hiss of marram grass on bare legs, the tease of perfumes and scents like none he had known before. Exotic, heady, powerful. His mind was spinning; he could see nothing beyond the pressing throng of bodies. But that didn't matter. He didn't want to see beyond. The rest of the world no longer had meaning.

*Just... stay indoors. Promise me Jack?*

Moira's voice again, but distantly. Further away than the

sea beyond the dunes but audible still. Part of him thought he should cling to those words, like driftwood on a vast ocean, the only thing he could hang on to. But it was a part of him that was deep inside his mind, too deep to have any bearing on what was happening.

And what *was* happening?

Beautiful young women appearing out of the mist to take him into the dunes. It didn't really seem likely, did it? Even in this unlikely place of unlikely things.

A dream? That must be it. Just a dream. He would wake up soon, maybe he wouldn't even remember it. So best just let the dreaming take him and embrace him in its grasp, let its current carry him where it would. It didn't matter. Nothing mattered...

He was lying on the sand, staring up into the dark, faintly glowing mist-infused night sky. How had he gotten here? That didn't matter either, these things happened in dreams. He was naked he realised, but not cold, not really. He felt the damp touch of the mist upon his skin but there was no discomfort.

The singing had stopped. All he could hear was the sea, faint as sighs, lost out in the night.

Where had the women gone? This wasn't how his dream was supposed to end. It was *his* dream after all.

He tried to sit up, but he'd no strength for it. He let his head slump to the side, feeling the sand cling to his cheek. They were still with him, kneeling in the sand. Watching him silently. Dimly, beyond, he could make out the towering forms of the driftwood pillars. He was back atop Mount Dune.

It had been a far easier climb this time…

As one, they dropped to all fours and began crawling towards him. They were laughing, but not the playful laughter of earlier. This was a deep, dry, snickering coming from the black pit of their throats.

It was the jabbering cackle of Burrows-Things.

Of course, that's what they were.

He'd known that, hadn't he?

He supposed he had. But it didn't matter. They were beautiful and they wanted him. What else did he have anyway? A wife he didn't love, a job he didn't want, a life that had become a façade behind which lay only dead, stale air and forgotten dreams. At least until he'd met Moira, but she had run off and left him. The family business. More important than him. So, let them come to him and take what they wanted.

He felt their hands upon him. Their mouths upon him. Their skin, as soft and delicate and dry as antique sand, against his. Desire filled him again. It gave him purpose and meaning and use. Probably theirs rather than his, but, at least, it didn't leave him filled with the cloying emptiness of another morning knowing today would be the same as yesterday and the same as tomorrow.

They were offering him their love and it was all-consuming.

He felt one of them straddle him as other hands pressed down upon him, hard enough for him to feel his body sinking into the sand. A mouth was pressed against his, it was warm, but not wet. It tasted as dry as ashes. He wanted to splutter and force his mouth away, but couldn't move, even if he had the strength too many hands held him. Strong, long-fingered hands gripped his head. Something was running into his mouth, down his throat, becoming part of him. Sand. That was what it was. Sand was passing from her mouth to his. He shouldn't be able to breathe. But he found he still could. He felt his cock being taken into something, like the mouth kissing sand it was warm but completely dry. There was momentary resistance, then acceptance and something cackled, a maniacal howl of animalistic pleasure.

Sand was all about him, enveloping and consuming him. He was going to die he realised, but he didn't struggle. There was no point. It would do no good. Besides he still had his lust to expel, he still –

There was light, blinding white and scouring. The air was filled with screeching cries and scurrying limbs as the pressure upon his body was released. He managed to roll onto his side and gagged up great wet globs of sand as tears rolled down his cheeks.

His senses swam and blackness rushed in upon him. Before he slipped away, through tear-blurred eyes, he saw a pair of battered red baseball boots and distantly a voice sighed.

"Why the fuck couldn't you just stay in the house..."

Then the world went away.

# Seventeen

They walked in silence along the shoreline.

The sun had scattered a million diamonds to dance and shimmer upon the sea's swells and troughs. Moira stopped, her eyes narrowing against the glare as a faint smile brushed her lips. She felt for his hand without looking. Jack returned the little squeeze as he followed her gaze, something jumped from the water, a momentary flash of quicksilver against the molten water. A dolphin? Maybe something else?

Jack suspected something else though he didn't ask. He suspected there was an awful lot of something elses here.

He carried a bottle of water in his free hand and he slipped his fingers from Moira's to take off the cap and swig deeply. His mouth still felt gritty. He offered it to Moira, but she shook her head. His hand found hers again and he let their fingers entwine.

She turned from the sea, her grey eyes held his, watchful, glinting, restless. The wind teased licks of black hair across her face. She left them to dance and reached up to kiss him. A brief caress, then she pulled away, gave his hand a little tug and they continued to walk barefooted across the glistening sand.

*Do you, really?*

Yeah. He did. Really.

He'd awoken back in the White Room with bright sunlight pushing at the window.

He'd lain there, listening to the morning lament of faraway gulls, and decided it must just have been a dream. Beautiful women carrying him away in the night. Obviously just a dream.

He'd stretched out and felt the sand granulating the sheets around him. His mouth had tasted of ashes. Then he'd smelt bacon frying.

He'd tried to get out of bed, but found he'd no strength and had fallen back onto the sand smeared cotton.

After a while, the sound of singing had drifted up, a woman's voice, but she wasn't singing a strange, haunting song of love and desire. She was singing *White Riot*, accompanied by a vigorous assault on every saucepan in the kitchen by the sound of it.

"Moira?"

His voice wasn't even a croak. There was water on the bedside table and he gulped it down even when it hurt his throat and he kept swallowing while it dribbled down his chin. By the time the glass was empty, he was breathless and had slumped back onto the pillows exhausted.

A little later, he wasn't sure how long as he'd drifted off into a brief floating doze, Moira appeared, sitting on the edge of the bed. She was wearing cut down denim shorts and her *Ramones* t-shirt, even though the house was cold enough to chill Jack beneath the sheets. She looked unutterably beautiful.

"How you feeling, lover boy?"

"Incapable..." he replied after consideration, "...of

anything."

"I think I can help you with that," she'd produced a plate stacked with a mountain of bacon sandwiches and a long glass of cold orange juice.

"I used all the bacon," Jack muttered a hoarse rasp, his stomach gurgling in anticipation.

Moira handed him the juice before squirming under the sheets beside him.

"I got some more."

"How?"

"I... erm... know a shortcut to the shops."

"There's a *shortcut?* There's a *shop?*"

Moira winked at him as she'd torn an entirely unladylike mouthful off her first sandwich.

Jack knew bacon sandwiches came before most things in life, and they'd ate in comfortable silence, sitting up in bed, legs pressing lightly against each other.

The sandwiches were possibly the most delicious thing he'd ever eaten and the juice tasted like nectar, sweet and soothing upon his raw throat.

Moira let out a long sigh when they were done, running her finger through a smear of grease on the plate and licking it off her finger. When she was done, she hooked an arm around him and snuggled up.

"Moira where have you been? What is this place? What happened to me last-"

She reached up and pressed a finger against his lips, he could still smell the bacon grease on it.

"Later... just hold me for a bit, old man."

Jack twisted around and they slipped down the bed, her

hair splaying across his chest as she rested her head upon it.

"Shouldn't we be going?"

Moira didn't answer for a while and when she did it was just a breath.

"No... not just yet. Not just yet."

And then she was asleep.

\*

They sat on dry sand further up the beach, watching the waves and listening to their refrain. The sun was lowering toward the ocean beneath a mackeraled sky

"Why couldn't I leave?" he asked eventually, unable to hold his questions any longer. They'd slept most of the day and when he'd tried to ask again after they woke Moira had slipped from the bed and said they should go for a walk. He had a whole list of questions to work through, but that one seemed as good a place as any to start.

She continued to stare at the sea.

"You said something about crossing the circle?" He prompted when she didn't answer.

"You gave yourself to them. You crossed the circle of your own free will. That's the deal. You accepted their enchantment and it tied you to this place. It tied you to the Fey."

"The Fey? Is that them? The Burrows-Things?"

"No," Moira shook her head, still not looking at him, "They're Sand-Waifs. The less charitable call them Sand-Hags."

"They were hideous at first, then beautiful..."

"Their beauty is an illusion, kind of... but here the margin between the illusion and the actual is much thinner than it is back in the Real."

"The Real?"

"Your world."

Jack looked across the beach, which was as bereft of humanity as usual.

"This isn't my world?"

"Well..." she sighed "...it's complicated."

"Try me. Some people say I'm quite bright."

Moira's eyes darted towards him, "They do?"

He nudged her with his elbow and once her eyes had slid back to the sea, she went on.

"The Real is the weft, the Fey is the warp and together they make the Weave."

Jack raised an eyebrow.

"The Weave of the World," Moira offered, by way of explanation, "neither can exist without the other, entwined, but invisible to each other, binding the Weave. Most things are unable to cross from one to the other, or even be aware the other exists, beyond their dreams at least. Too anchored and connected to either the weft or the warp, to The Real or The Fey."

Jack stared at her, "I thought you were a punk, not a hippy?"

Moira laughed.

"So... here, in the *Fey*, that's where the monsters live?"

"Monsters?"

"The... Sand-Waifs?"

"They're not really monsters."

Jack was unconvinced, "What are they then?"

"Creatures of magic... for want of a better phrase."

"Creatures of magic?"

"Yeah... like me."

"Like you?"

"I'm Fey, Jack, of this world, not yours."

"But, you like *The Ramones*, and pork scratchings and pints of cider and..."

"Mortal men."

She took his hand and squeezed it.

"And there was me thinking it was just older guys you liked."

"You're not old."

"Older than you."

"Jack... you have no idea..."

He stared inquiringly at her, but her eyes had slid back to the sea and the colours the setting sun was casting upon its churning, restless surface.

If they'd been back in London, supping pints in a smoky pub in between throwing coins into the jukebox he would have dismissed her explanation as nothing more than happy-clappy bullshit. But he'd seen too much for that, even if his mind was still flailing about unable to accept her story entirely.

"So... if these two worlds are entwined but invisible to each other. How'd we get here?"

"Because we're both disconnected souls. We have broken the anchors holding us to the warp and the weft so we can encompass the whole of the Weave."

"I'm not sure I get that..."

"I became disconnected a long time ago; I embraced it and am, now, something of a master of it. For you, it is still happening. You can't do it freely, or see the paths and ways, the threads and the knots yet. But you're disconnected enough for me to take you through."

"Is that why I couldn't drive out of here."

"No. As I said, that was the Sand-Waif's enchantment. Without that, you could go back the way you came through. But I doubt very much you could find your way back here again alone. If you leave, you leave."

"So, we could go now?"

Moira shook her head, "No, I'll have to break their enchantment first."

"You can do that?"

"Yes. Tonight. I'll do what needs to be done."

"And what does that entail?"

Moira twisted around and placed a hand on his cheek, before slipping her fingers around the back of his neck and pulling him towards her.

"Too many questions... just shut up and kiss me."

So Jack did and all the questions slid from his mind. For a little while at least.

# Eighteen

They headed back towards the dunes, arms about each other's waists, once the globe of the sun had slipped beneath a sea turned to molten gold in the day's last light

The curve rising from Moira's hip to her waist was a graceful arc that magnetically drew his hand; it fit so perfectly he'd considered it almost magical. Not the only thing magical about her either, it now appeared.

Jack eyed The Burrows as they drew close. Sensing him stiffen Moira dug her fingers gently into his side. When he glanced at her, she gave him a little smile that said everything would be good. Her smiles always made him feel like that anyway, but he knew what she meant.

There was nothing to fear when he was with her.

"Why did you leave?" Jack asked again, after a while.

Moira slipped from his grasp and plucked a dried stem of grass half buried in the fine sand where the dunes began to rise from the beach. The grass had sprouted a seed head and her thumb run along its bristles as they continued to walk.

"My father sent me a message, I had to go. Trouble with my sister. Family business."

"You have a sister?"

"Several."

"I didn't know... you never said."

"I try not to think about them. But some things bind even the disconnected; he sent me a message in the storm, in the rhymes of its thunder. I knew it must be serious to go to so much trouble. I had to leave immediately; I was summoned, so to speak. There wasn't time to warn you."

"He sent you a message in a *storm?*"

Moira gave a little shrug, "He's never liked the phone."

"Who is your father?"

"A difficult and extraordinary man not overly impressed by wayward daughters."

"Is everything ok?"

Moira flashed him a smile, which was something that usually chased all things from his mind, but this one was transitory and bitter-sweet.

"Matters have been resolved, for now," there was coldness in her tone, an alien thread of iron running through in her usually soft voice. She returned her attention to twirling the grass stem between her fingers.

She didn't want to say more and he let it rest, she would explain it to him in her own good time if she wanted to. If she didn't, no matter. He was too pleased to have her back to even really care what she was or who she was. He loved her and she made him happy in a way he could not find the words to express. Nothing else really mattered.

"I saw a woman on the beach," Jack said, still fishing for answers he could stack in his head in a way that made some sense, "except she was a kind of ghost... I could see through her and then she faded away... was she really a ghost?"

"No. This is a kissing point. A place where the Real and the Fey are closest and they mirror each other. In other places, the two worlds are utterly different. There is a beach just like this in your world, except it has a holiday park at one end and the woods have been cut down and slicks of oil dirty the sand and... Well, I prefer this one."

"And the woman I saw was... on *that* beach?"

Moira nodded, "Some people can flit between the worlds without realising. Others spend half their lives in silence and solitude trying to disconnect and never manage it," she shrugged, "there's no rhyme or reason to it."

Moira slipped her hand into his and stared at him, "Do you believe what I'm telling you."

"A couple of days ago I would have laughed at you. Now..."

"Now?"

"Now, I've seen too much. Far too much."

Moira squeezed his hand and he squeezed it back.

"Why did you bring me here?" He asked as much to fill the silence with something other than the hiss of the wind through the tossing marram grass.

"Because the Feylands are my home, because they are beautiful, because I wanted to know..."

"Know what?"

She lifted her gaze from the grass and stared at him. She had beautiful eyes, he'd always thought, framed in the thick dark eyeliner she permanently wore. Grey as morning mist, but with the faintest fissures of blue crackling around her pupils. With her jet-black hair, she should have had dark eyes to match, but he'd never thought too much about it because he tended to lose the thread of any thought if he looked into them for long enough. Only now did he realise just how otherworldly and ethereal they were. Eyes that suggested they saw more than they should, eyes that had seen things he could not comprehend. Fey eyes.

"To know you better. To know your soul better."

"And there was me thinking you just wanted my body," he gave a little laugh, but it faded into the wind when Moira didn't smile.

"Because I love you."

Jack stopped, the encroaching weight of the surrounding Burrows forgotten.

"You do?"

Moira turned back towards him, "You're a kind man with a good heart. You make me happy. That's a rare gift, a gift few across the Weave have ever given me."

He blushed and looked away, suddenly embarrassed for reasons he couldn't entirely fathom.

"There's nothing particularly special about me... you, on the other hand, could have whoever you want."

"True," Moira's familiar twisting grin returned to her lips, "but I want you. I know you think you are nothing special Jack, I know you've never understood why I came over to you in the bookshop that day."

"I'd assumed it was just animal lust?"

"You're like a rock pool, Jack, dark still water reflecting the world away, but down at the bottom, between the kelp and the shadows, I see the things that glitter in you."

"I think you're very nice too..."

Moira laughed, reached up, curled a hand around his

neck and pulled him towards her lips, the dry husk of the grass stem scratching his skin as they kissed.

*

"You don't have to go back. You could stay here. With me."

They lay facing each other in bed, heads resting on crumpled pillows, arms and legs entwined.

"In the House of Shells?"

"Why not?"

"I thought it was a holiday let?"

Moira raised one perfectly arched eyebrow, "You said something earlier about being bright?"

Jack smiled and swept a turn of hair from Moira's face, tucking it gently behind her ear. She really did have the softest hair.

"I noticed the old photograph, your grandmother I assumed. I could see the resemblance so I guess this place has been in your family for a while?"

Moira smiled, "For a while..."

"It is your grandmother, isn't it?"

She stared at him for a bit and then kissed him softly by way of an answer.

"Stay with me, Jack."

"I... can't Moira, you know..."

"You're married. Yes. But you're not happy, there's nothing there for you and that's why you are disconnecting from The Real. One of the reasons anyway. Your life is so short, please don't waste it."

Would he be happy here, in this strange place with this

beautiful young woman? Of course he would, but... but what? Would it be so hard, really?

"I can't just... not go back. I would have to see Amanda first. I can't just phone Amanda up and-"

"You can't phone. Not from here."

"Then I'd have to go back first and see her. Tell her. Explain to her..."

Moira rolled onto her back and stared at the shadow engulfed ceiling.

"If you go, you won't come back. Even if you think you want to. Stay or go, there's no other choice."

"She's my wife. My friend. I loved her once."

"Do you love her now?"

He supposed he answered that question by not answering it at all.

Moira let out a long sigh before shuffling off the sheets and climbing out of bed.

"Where are you going?"

"To the dunes, I have to get the Sand-Waifs to break their enchantment."

"Is that... dangerous?"

Moira sat on the edge of the bed and pulled on her t-shirt, "No, they can't harm me."

"But they can me?"

Moira shook her head and looked back over her shoulder, "They mean you no harm, they only want to mate with you."

"Mate with me?"

"They need a man for that, Sand-Waifs are only born female."

175

"So, if you hadn't come back last night..."

"They'd still be fucking you."

"Oh."

Moira laughed, "Yeah, I know. I saved you from a fate worse than death, being screwed senseless by a dozen beautiful women." She twisted around and kissed him on the forehead, "You can thank me later."

"Well, they weren't *really* beautiful."

"You wouldn't have known the difference, their scent is... hypnotic and you've been exposed to it for long enough for it never to wear off."

"And when they'd finished... *mating* with me? Would they have eaten me or something?"

"No... you'd have been free to go. Half starved, dehydrated and sore from head to toe, but you'd probably have survived."

"Probably?"

"They're quite demanding creatures. Some women are..." Moira jumped up and pulled on her jeans.

"Lucky you came back when you did."

"Not luck, Kalla called me, told me what was happening."

"Kalla?"

Moira waved a hand in front of her, "The House of Shells. She's alive."

Jack looked uncertainly about him, "She is?"

"Kalla is her spirit, she's been looking after you. Keeping an eye on you for me."

"That's how the washing up got done?"

Moira shook her head, "So the only thing you noticed

176

about this house was the bloody washing up getting done? Men!"

"The Giggle-finch…"

"The…?"

"I kept hearing a girl giggling. That was the House?"

Moira nodded, "She has a pretty limited vocabulary, but everything in the House comes from Kalla… the light, water, heat, even getting rid of the sewage."

Jack stared at Moira, "You're telling me you have your own shit fairy?"

A lilting giggle floated up from somewhere in the house and he pulled a face.

"No offence."

"Don't worry, Kalla likes you," Moira bent over and kissed his forehead, "She has crap taste in men too…"

"And the phone? It's not connected to anything. That's Kalla?"

"It's not really a phone. It just looks like a phone. Nothing here is what it seems. It's just an illusion. Like the Sand-Waif's beauty."

He sat up a little straighter, "Then what is it, really?"

"Some things you don't need to know. The House of Shells cares and protects those it loves. Like me. And now you. She kept a watch on you and tried to stop you leaving the house last night."

"She did?"

"She slammed the door in your face a couple of times, but the Sand-Waif's enchantment was too strong for that to wake you."

"And she's been watching me all the time?"

Moira pulled on her leather jacket (which he guessed Kalla must have retrieved from the dunes) and glanced back at him, "Don't worry, your secrets are safe with her. She's very discreet. Really."

He remembered curling up with Moira's t-shirt around a pillow.

Another giggle tinkled faintly and Moira winked at him.

"Erm... do you need me to come with you?"

She stared at him, her eyes narrowing pointedly, "Probably best you stay here tonight...."

"Yeah... probably."

Moira left the room without turning on the light and Jack lay there, listening to her move around downstairs. When he heard the front door shut behind her, he went to the window.

He watched her head towards the trees in long, confident strides, the studs on her battered leather jacket reflecting the light cast from the House of Shells. He could make out the lithe forms of beautiful young women in the trees waiting for her.

As Moira approached them, they bowed their heads and dropped to their knees, only moving once she had strode through them, rising to hurry after her until they were all consumed within the night.

.

# Nineteen

Jack sat in the Cortina, drumming his fingers on the wheel as he stared out at the dark grey tarmac of the road. Despite all of Moira's assurances, he'd fully expected he'd just arrive back at the House of Shells again. Even when she'd hugged him fiercely and placed a fleeting kiss on his lips that smacked of finality.

"Go," she'd said, and returned to the cottage without a backwards glance.

He could still smell her perfume.

He closed his eyes and took a few breaths, deep and slow, fingers still tapping. He just had to nudge the car forward and turn back on to the sane, solid tarmac and he would be free of the House of Shells, the Burrows-Things, the beach and all the strangeness of The Fey. He would be back in his world.

Back in the Real.

Jack pushed open the door and climbed out, settling his feet in the mulch of wet leaves carpeting the lane.

There was the faintest shimmer, he noticed, between the lane and road. As if he saw it through a thin veneer of water.

Back into the Real. Never to return.

"I'll see you in London when you get back?" He'd asked over breakfast when Moira had told him she wouldn't be coming with him.

"I can't," she'd said, cradling a mug of tea.

"But when you've finished here, you'll be coming home?"

"This is home, Jack."

"But you live in Fulham."

She'd smiled, seemingly despite herself, then shook her head hard enough for her long black hair to flick about her face.

"I can't go back to the Real... not for a long while at least."

"Why not? I thought you could move freely between the two?"

"Not anymore."

Jack had frowned, not understanding.

"A price had to be paid for the Sand-Waifs to break their enchantment, Jack. You can go, but I have to stay here in the Fey."

"They want to mate with you?"

"Did your parents ever give you that talk about the birds and the bees?"

"Erm... they weren't really good at that kinda stuff. Wrong generation."

"Even so, your rudimentary grasp of biology should be sufficient to know that isn't why they want me."

"Then why?"

"My blood is sacred. It has power. They want me close... they mean me no harm, but I cannot leave the Fey anymore."

"Forever?"

"No, not forever. Just a little while."

"Then you'll be coming back to London at some point?"

"Eventually. Probably."

"Then get in touch when you do, please."

"I won't be able to."

"Why not?"

Moira had carefully placed her mug in front of her, "Because you'll be dead."

He'd looked at her blankly. It was a look he'd found he'd become increasingly proficient at pulling off.

"I can't leave the Fey until you die, Jack."

"But... that's..."

"You wanted to go home. I can't keep you here a prisoner so I can have my freedom. That was the Sand-Waif's deal."

"But I can come back here, couldn't I?"

"In theory."

"Theory?"

"Only disconnected souls can move between the weft and the warp. You could disconnect completely, but... I don't think you can. Not enough to find your own way back anyway."

"How would I?"

"Cut yourself off from everything that ties you to the Real. Everything you love and cherish, every responsibility, every ambition, every hope. Everything anchoring you to that world. Then... maybe you could find your way back."

"Maybe?"

"Maybe. Not everyone can. Many have spent decades on top of mountains or in remote caves trying to disconnect from the Real without ever coming close..."

She'd reached over and taken his hand. "I know you love me Jack, but you don't want to stay. You still love your wife, you're too anchored in the Real. So, go back to London and

Amanda and live your life. I'll be fine."

"This is… it?"

"I guess so."

"But you're trapped here on this beach…"

"No, just in the Fey. It's a whole world. My world. I haven't given up so much. Though punk hasn't really taken off here, I'll manage."

He hadn't known what to say, so Moira had pulled him to his feet and taken him by the hand to his waiting car. Hugged him and kissed him goodbye.

*You could stay here. With me*

Why was he leaving?

Would it be so wrong if he just stayed here, disappeared from the Real and… and let the world wonder what had become of him. Leave Amanda wondering what had become of him for the rest of her life. Never knowing if he'd run away somewhere or was buried in an unmarked grave or had lost his memory or any of the other possibilities that accounted for a human being disappearing from the face of the Earth.

He'd loved Amanda once. Until recently he thought he still did. He'd a good job, friends, relatives, he'd a life. It was one thing to walk away from it, it was another to let all the people that cared for him think he was dead, or worse.

*Wasn't it?*

He turned back and looked along the lane, the sun was bright, and its light dappled the leaf covered track through the overhanging canopy of rusting leaves. He couldn't see the House of Shells or Moira, but he knew she was there and if he drove back into the Real he would never, ever see her again.

He'd been desperate to get away from this place, but now it tugged at him. It was beautiful, but, of course, it wasn't the beach or the sea, the dunes or the woods calling him. They were but the frame for Moira and a life he could have.

But was it enough? To give up *everything*. He wanted her. He craved her, he wanted to lose himself in those strange, knowing misty-grey eyes of hers. He wanted to be happy.

But was it enough to give up everything for?

As he looked down the lane, two golden butterflies emerged from the trees. They cavorted about each other before returning to the shadows of the trees, leaving a momentary fizzy trail of honey-light behind them. The same pair he'd seen up by the pond, he supposed.

Butterglows, Moira had called them. She'd looked at him strangely when he'd mentioned them and squeezed his hand. The creatures spent their entire lives as a pair. If they were separated, they both died, when one died the other would die too. Inseparable they lived their lives playing and cavorting together under the light of another sun. A sun that shone only upon them. Moira had smiled and told him he was very lucky to see them. Few people did.

The saying went that only those truly in love ever did.

Slowly Jack climbed back behind the wheel and closed the door. After a moment, he nudged the car forward onto the road. There was no jar or judder, no sense of anything unusual or untoward to mark his passing from the Fey back into the Real.

The world did blur and shimmer more noticeably for a time, but that was simply because he was crying.

# Twenty

Jack had never really believed in God, though, admittedly, he'd never believed in magical worlds, strange beasties or houses that did the washing up for you either and he'd been wrong about them. He had, however, always harboured a sneaking suspicion the world was arranged in such a way that it would never pass up an opportunity to fuck you over.

The drive back to London had been uneventful other than the feeling of gloom that settled inexorably upon him, a weight incrementally growing with each mile of tarmac that disappeared beneath the Cortina's wheels. Every one taking him further and further from Moira, though she was already so far away he suspected mere miles could not measure the distance.

In unison with his mood the skies became ever more dark and oppressive. The rain started as he passed Reading and chased him all the way to his doorstep, reducing the world to grubby, blurred smears behind the traffic spray.

He had been so eager to escape the House of Shells, but the world he'd returned to seemed smaller and dirtier, choking on its own bitter fumes, faceless and inhuman. Drab buildings housing drab lives and blank-eyed souls blinded from the wonder of the world.

He missed the smell of the sea and shriek of the gulls. He

missed the beat of the waves and the texture of the sand. He missed the wind hissing through the marram grass and the stillness within the trees. He missed the taste of salt on his lips. He missed everything, but most of all he missed Moira.

His house looked no different from the one he'd left. A neat, suburban terrace bereft of climbing ivy and monsters at the end of the garden that wanted to hump him within half an inch of his life. But it looked smaller, somehow, and it exuded a greyness that had nothing to do with the dirty, cold rain slicking its roof and pebble-dashed walls.

Inside, it had the strange familiarity that always haunted a home after a holiday or some other extended absence from the norm. And Jack guessed he'd been about as absent from the norm as it was possible to get.

A small pile of official-looking brown envelopes and other sundry unwanted crap littered the doormat. He tossed them aside after a brief automated shuffle and slumped into his armchair in the living room. Amanda had the sofa, he had the armchair.

Had they ever discussed that particular arrangement?

They'd been a time when they'd always shared the sofa together, but at some point, in the years since they'd married and bought the house they'd expected to start their family in, the armchair had become his; a padded beige throne from which to rule his castle.

Or a comfortably upholstered banishment from his wife's affections?

The silence was as complete as anything offered in the House of Shells, but it wasn't the silence of solitude and remoteness, it was a heavy, sombre silence that pervaded the house like a dampening fog.

He put the TV on to try and fill the void, but he managed less than thirty seconds of *Scooby-Do* before killing it.

*Damn those pesky kids...*

Reluctantly he checked for messages, Amanda had planned to phone the previous night from Spain. It wasn't a huge problem, there were plenty of washable excuses; he'd gone out, he'd got home late from work, he'd almost become a stud for a coven of Sand-Hags. There was always a plausible explanation. Still, the blinking red light on the answering machine had an accusingly angry insistence about it.

*Where were you, Jack? Where were you?*

His finger hovered over the play button; he didn't want to hear Amanda's voice. He'd never felt guilty about Moira, other than perhaps feeling guilty for not feeling guilty. He'd never expected to be unfaithful to his wife and never had been before. He'd always felt contempt for the guys in the office bragging about their infidelities as they clutched their post-work pints above their beer guts.

He wasn't like that. He loved his wife. He was lucky. They were lucky. Everything was going to be good. Always would be. Except it hadn't turned out that way and it hadn't been for years.

She'd become cold and distant. Not a sudden thing, but a quiet, slow process that had begun the day the doctor had told them they couldn't have children. More precisely told them *he* couldn't have children.

Amanda had hugged him afterwards and told him it didn't matter. Worse things happen at sea, she'd said it with a little smile that had made him glance away as it only magnified the sadness in her eyes.

But it *had* mattered.

They never talked about it again. Not in the eight years since they'd come out of the hospital and he'd managed to keep his face even till they got home and he could lock himself in the toilet. Even then he'd had to bite his knuckles to stifle the sobs. Stupid really. Nobody had died, he'd thought at the time though that hadn't entirely been true.

Their marriage had started its slow demise that day; the silence filling the house had filled their marriage too. They had never argued or fought. You needed heat for that and their marriage hadn't been ripped apart by competing passions. It had frozen in a thousand unreturned gestures and petty indifferences until all they did was orbit each other in the same space, circling, but never touching and he'd eventually become the same as the men he despised.

Still, he'd come home, hadn't he?

He could have stayed with Moira, but he'd come home. Back to this silent house and the blinking, accusing red eye of the answering machine. He owed Amanda that much, didn't he? He couldn't just have stayed with Moira without an explanation? A goodbye? Something?

No, of course, he couldn't. Even if it meant he would never see Moira again. He couldn't have done that.

Jack stabbed the button, listened to the click and hiss of the tape followed by his own stilted greeting and invitation to leave a message after the beep and waited for his wife's voice. It would be flat and perfunctory. There would be no curiosity as to why he wasn't home, no I miss yous, no I love yous, no see you soons. Those things had withered away a long time ago.

As it was there was only one message and it wasn't from Amanda.

*"Hey... erm...It's Bill. Really sorry about all this, I guess you must be pissed off as hell, but... well, these things happen. We'll have to talk when we get back and sort things out... amicably as we can. Really sorry... it just happened..."*

Jack frowned, played the message back and then deleted it. Had to be a wrong number. The only Bill he knew was one of the partners at work and though it did sound a little like him, he couldn't imagine why he'd be leaving cryptic apologetic messages on their answering machine.

The message instantly forgotten - he already had enough bouncing around the inside of his head after all - he grabbed his bag and wandered through to the kitchen with the intention of stuffing his sand-soiled clothes into the washing machine.

His eye fell on the envelope almost immediately.

The round breakfast table under the window had been swept clean of everything else, which was unusual in itself as the table served as their receptacle for all manner of short-term clutter.

He placed his bag down on the linoleum-tiled floor and stared at the table. He hadn't tidied the table up before he'd left. Tidying up had never been one of his more reliable virtues and even less so when he'd been hurriedly rushing from the house in the early hours to pick Moira up. There hadn't been much of anything in his head other than the prospect of spending whole days with Moira.

Amanda had taken a cab to Gatwick the morning before and it didn't seem likely a burglar had broken into clear their breakfast table of the old magazines, takeaway menus, receipts and scrawled grocery lists that usually carpeted it.

And he was damn sure *this* house didn't tidy up after him.

*Jack*, the envelope said, unmistakably in Amanda's neat, precise hand.

He sat down at the table and turned the envelope over a couple of times before tearing it open and unfolding the single white sheet of heavy stationery inside.

*Jack*

*I'm leaving you.*

*Sorry to be so blunt, but I can't face telling you in person so I've taken the cowards way out and left this letter. I didn't go to Gatwick yesterday and I'm not going to see Mum. I'm going to be away for a couple of weeks with Bill. Hopefully, by then we can sort out the things we need to. We both know this should have happened a while ago, but now things have come to a head and it's for the best.*

*I know you've been seeing someone too, Bill told me you took leave and aren't going to any conference. I think I knew anyway. You've been happier these last few months. I hope it works out for you too, whoever she is, and that we can do this without any bitterness.*

*You should also know that I'm pregnant.*

*Take care.*

*Amanda*

Jack read the letter twice before refolding it and sliding it back into the envelope. He wondered if he should be angry. When that didn't come, he wondered just how he should feel.

Bill Fisher? *Bill bloody Fisher?*

They'd been to a few of those obligatory soul-crushing firm dinner parties. The ones where everyone smiled patronisingly at each other, laughed uproariously at crap jokes and tried to cut the professional throats of their colleagues as soon as they looked away. Amanda had never seemed to enjoy them any more than he had. He was surprised she'd even remembered Bill's name.

Big, blustering, red-faced, Bill Fisher, who was older than him, fatter than him, balder than him and had a pudgy, misshapen nose that looked like it had been thrown onto his face by a drunken potter. Richer than him sure, but otherwise, what did he have that would have attracted Amanda? Apart from a healthy sperm count.

He sat back in the chair and stared at the envelope. Then he laughed and kept laughing till tears rolled down his face.

He'd given up the woman he loved so he could come back and tell Amanda to her face that it was time for them to split up. So that she wouldn't have to lay awake at night tormented by wondering just what had happened to him. And she'd beat him to it. With a Dear John letter and a bun in the oven.

Jack threw back his head and laughed some more.

As he'd always suspected, the world never missed an opportunity to fuck you over.

# Twenty-One

It was another forty-eight hours before he left home for the last time.

He'd gone into work the morning after reading Amanda's letter and resigned. From the way people refused to meet his eye, he suspected he may not have been the first one in the office to find out about Bill Fisher and Amanda. He was sure it was quite the scandal.

He remembered Bill had split up from his wife, a too-thin woman who never spoke a sentence of more than five words, a few months earlier. He hadn't thought anything about it at the time; he'd erroneously thought it was none of his business.

Mr Keats had asked him to think about things, not to make any hasty decisions, difficult times, etc. Take some leave, dear boy. He'd need to work his notice anyway. Act in haste, repent at leisure, eh, old chap? Think about all those years he'd served the firm.

Jack had sat across from his portly boss who tended to peer at the world through a squint of disdain and politely listened to him trot out his clichés. When Mr Keats had finally run out of ways to tell him the firm was more important than such a trifling thing as a marriage, he'd stood up and told him he wasn't going to spend another second working for a firm where one of the partners had fucked and impregnated his wife. He wasn't working any notice and they could stick their references up their collective arse. He was leaving the country.

"Leaving the country?" Mr Keats had blinked at him from behind his thick horn-rimmed glasses with the look of a man who'd heard rumours about these strange lands beyond the English Channel, but who was at a complete loss as to understand why a man might want to visit any of them.

"Might as well travel the world," Jack had spat, "nothing for me here anymore." Then he'd stormed out.

He thought he'd done a good job of looking like the aggrieved husband burning with anger and resentment. One bridge burned. One thing disconnected.

He'd spent the rest of the time on the phone, explaining to his brother Dave, cousin Kev and assorted friends what had happened and that he was going travelling for a while. Quite a long while.

He didn't like the concern in their voices. The worry, the commiserations and sympathies, all the anything-I-can-do-mates, but he let them wash over him. He was going to travel and build a new life abroad. It wasn't a lie. Not really. And maybe one day he really would be in touch. Maybe he would visit. But he didn't think so.

He had to let his anchors go, all of them, if he was ever to get back to Moira. And he wanted that more than anything he'd ever wanted in his life. Every moment he was away from her burnt and twisted him, hollowed him and buried him. He wanted to hold her tight to him again, and never let her go. She was the only thing in the world he wanted. Even if she wasn't in the same world at all.

He took a long time writing a letter to Amanda, which he left on the breakfast table next to hers. In the end, he kept it brief. He told her he wished her well and he was going abroad. She could have the house and everything in it, he wouldn't need it and he didn't want the memories.

He wrote goodbye at the bottom and then his name.

It looked a lot like a suicide note to Jack. Perhaps it was. Perhaps that's what she'd think it was.

He went to the bank the next morning and took half the cash in their joint account and everything from his own savings. Not something a man planning to kill himself would do, hopefully, she'd realise. He didn't want her to think she'd driven him to take his own life. Just that she'd driven him to run far away.

He took most of his clothes, filled the Cortina with them and posted the house keys through the letterbox. He'd been so excited when they'd bought that house. When it had finally been theirs and they'd walked into it, unfurnished, uncarpeted and smelling of paint and new wallpaper and possibilities. He and Amanda were going to be so happy and everything was going to be perfect.

He remembered Amanda beaming at him that day, utterly unable to keep the smile from her face. Her long blonde hair rippling down her back as she'd rushed from room to room. Years later she'd had her hair cropped short, it'd made her look severe and cold he'd always thought. She'd cut it not long after they'd found out he could never father a child. He told himself there was no connection; she was just changing her image and wanted to look more professional for work. But more than just her hair changed over those months and years.

She'd cut her smile short too.

He climbed into the car without a backward glance.

He drove a few miles till he found a charity shop and dumped most of his clothes on them. He wasn't sure how much personal possessions anchored him to the Real, but he wasn't taking any chances.

Then he drove west and hoped he'd done enough.

*

It hadn't been that long, but the air felt colder, the trees barer and the skies heavier than he remembered. And everything seemed to have faded a little, like a photograph left in the sunlight.

Hills rolled away on both sides of the grass verged road of intermittently pot-holed grey tarmac. A cow was making a racket somewhere out of sight, further away the familiar urgent cries of a gull, otherwise there was no sound bar the wind, his breath and the squeak of his boots on the road. They'd become familiar to him over the last week or so. His disconnecting serenade. He'd always hated unnecessary walking and had driven wherever possible, even if it was just to the corner shop to get milk and a weekend paper. Amanda had rolled her eyes and told him it was why he was getting fat.

What would she say now?

He'd left the Cortina in a long stay car park at Gatwick Airport, the keys dangling in the ignition and the door unlocked. If someone wanted it, they were welcome. People would think he'd jumped on a plane to Sydney or San Francisco or Timbuktu. And, eventually, they would forget about him.

Then he'd sat on a swaying train chugging westward, filled with the faint stink of dusty upholstery and cigarette smoke surrounded by blank-faced people reading books, newspapers or whatever stories passed behind their eyes.

He'd sat staring at nothing, trying to hear the pounding of the sea in the rattle of the rails and its sharp briny scent in the cheap acrid aftershave of a young man in an old suit sitting opposite him.

Jack found himself grasping for his memories, not only of the House of Shells, The Burrows and the long empty stretch of beach where the surf made his skin tingle and the memory of the sea was carved into the wet sand, but of Moira too. They all seemed indistinct, too blurred and unreal compared to the greasy blackheads clustered around the young man's broad, flattened nose, or the way the cellophane on his sandwich wrapper curled and flipped in rhythm to the jerks and shudders of the train.

He'd gotten off at the next stop. A small little strip of a station hedged in by trees. Nobody else got off and nobody else got on.

By his reckoning, he was still a hundred plus miles from the House of Shells.

He'd started walking and hadn't stopped till dusk, trudging along the side of the road, eyes fixed ahead, bag swaying at his side, ignoring the cars hissing by.

He had an envelope stuffed with cash. His life savings. His life's worth? He could feel the weight of it in his jacket pocket. Little bits of paper that men killed for. His mother, God rest her soul, would have been beside herself to know he was walking around with wads of banknotes, as if muggers had some kind of preternatural sense alerting them to the presence of cash-laden fools.

He'd sat in a pub and nursed a pint, the motoring atlas he'd brought with him spread out on the table. It turned out he'd a lot more than a hundred miles to go. He'd stared at the map, the web of coloured lines linking the amorphous towns and cities of Great Britain one to the other.

He'd asked if there was a bookshop nearby, the barmaid had frowned and given him some vague instructions into town where she thought there was a bookshop. Of some kind.

He'd hurried out and left his pint half-finished and his motoring atlas on the table.

He found the bookshop five minutes before it was due to close. A grey-haired woman kept a watchful eye on him as he sped along the shelves till he found the travel section. He'd wanted a walking guide, but instead found a comprehensive collection of Ordnance Survey maps and had bought the ones he needed to get him back to the House of Shells. Or rather the kissing point between The Real and The Fey.

He returned to the pub and plotted a route taking him back using only footpaths and back roads. Away from the noise and stink of the Twentieth century. As far away from the real world as possible.

It turned out the pub did rooms and he'd slept soundly and dreamed of Moira. He'd eaten a greasy breakfast and set out with the dawn.

A postbox stood just out of town, next to a wooden sign pointing towards a public footpath skirting a ploughed field before climbing towards a low fold of hills crowned with a copse of birch.

He shoved the envelope of money inside. He didn't need that any more either.

\*

A car passed, but it didn't slow. He'd been walking for days and he didn't look like the kind of man you stopped for anymore, even if he had been hitching. They sped by without a second glance.

Jack stared at it till it whizzed around a corner, going far too fast for a country back road. The tarmac felt strange beneath his feet, too hard, too real after days of wet earth and mulch, but there was no other path he could see to take him further and so he found himself back on the road he and Moira had driven down way back when in another life. His jeans were splattered with mud, the rain had soaked both him and the land several times in the last few days. How many days had it been?

He wasn't entirely sure.

Time had softened and bled into nothing but a record of steps taken. Each one closer to the House of Shells, each one further from the Real. Everything else had ceased to matter. He'd kept going on through whatever hours of daylight he was given and had blundered on in darkness when he'd a path that was broad enough to follow. He'd slept rough where he could, curled in any dry space he could find. In the damp when he couldn't.

The weight had fallen from him. Amanda had been right about walking. Though not eating much had probably played its part too. He'd kept a little money back for food, but he hadn't wanted to be distracted from the path and had made do with the last autumn blackberries and stream water as much as anything.

He felt lighter in his soul as well as his body, somehow. His work and marriage and home, plus all the other petty distractions of life, which had taken up so much of his mind for so long, had all been consumed in the bonfire of his commitments. All the people he knew, from his brother to the most casual of drinking companions in the pub darts team were behind him and ahead was... probably nothing at all. Though he had his hopes.

And he'd seen things as he'd walked.

Things he shouldn't have seen here in the Real; a young blonde woman, shimmering with summer light amongst the dying autumn trees, a shadow of something large falling across the sun accompanied by the beat of leathery wings, balls of crackling light the swirled around his head in a frenzied giddying dance. A beautiful white stallion across a field that looked, for all the world, like it had a single twisted horn protruding from its forehead. Sounds too, whispers and giggles and sighs in the darkness as if the trees and fields and hedgerows were trying to communicate with him.

Did he see into the Fey? Momentary glimpses across the Weave as he disconnected. Or just hallucinations brought on by exhaustion and lack of food.

He'd seen the butterglows again too. Several times, though only at dawn or dusk. Flitting around each other and leaving sparkling trails of gold to fade in their wake as they danced in the light of another sun. He thought they might be leading him back to the Fey, for they were always ahead of him and never behind. They didn't show themselves for long, but when they did, he found himself smiling a warm ghost of a smile until their light had faded back to nothing.

He didn't know if he would find his way back into the Feylands, back to Moira, but even if he didn't make it he felt a strange giddy sensation coursing through him. He was free. Free of all his burdens, as well as everything he'd never even considered to be a burden before.

Was it freedom he was feeling or was it how it felt to disconnect from the Real? He had nothing anymore. Not a wife, not a home, not a job, not a friend and not a penny to his name. He could do anything he chose. He didn't have to worry about a promotion or getting a new car or the next holiday or who to invite for Christmas or the fact Amanda had started to look at him in a way that suggested she was wondering what she'd ever seen in this fool in the first place.

None of it. He'd burned all those bridges and was left free to make any choice he wanted, to walk any road, to follow the weft and the warp of the Weave and see where it took him. He could do anything.

But there was only one thing he truly wanted anymore and she was just one more mile further along the road.

In another world entirely.

# Epilogue

Tchaikovsky didn't really suit sunshine.

She slipped back her hood and squinted up at the sky. The relentless drizzle had finally abated and a watery sun was brightening the clouds to the west. She thumbed her iPod before setting it to shuffle. Fantastic little gizmo, the iPod. She'd steadfastly refused to get a mobile phone, horrid things that people insisted on continually poking, prodding, fiddling and playing with in preference to having a life or a thought, but a little sliver of a box carrying all of your music, now that was clever.

She walked along the cliff tops, the music in her ears deafening her to both the cries of the wheeling gulls overhead and the waves smashing into the rocks far below. Now her hood was down the wind could tease her dark hair, though since she'd had it cut short and spiky that was less dramatic than it used to be.

The rain had stopped, but the wind was biting and few people were sharing the view with her. The chalk escarpments rolled along the coast down towards Eastbourne, where she'd started the day. She'd walked up to Beachy Head in the morning despite the rain. She found Eastbourne a drab, tired little town full of people waiting to die, but up here on the high rolling cliffs the views were long and beautiful and the air free of the crap folk insisted they needed to pump into it.

And up here the people who couldn't wait to die came.

The lost and unhappy, the broken and the bitter, the loveless and the too loved. Those who couldn't go on, those who didn't know how to go on, those that saw no reason to want to go on. The disconnected souls.

People came here from all over the world to undertake the ultimate disconnect.

So many came that chaplains patrolled the cliff tops to try and talk down those who had become so lost jumping off the highest sea cliff in England seemed preferable to drawing breath for another day.

She came here for much the same reason though she wasn't offering understanding, compassion or God's wisdom. She could offer something else, to the right person. A way out of this world well enough, but one that didn't involve throwing yourself off a cliff.

She followed the path along the folds of the hills towards the old Belle Tout lighthouse on the cliff tops. There was a middle-aged woman ahead, staring out to sea where the sun had poked through the clouds in several places to burnish patches of water from dull grey to dazzling silver.

The rain had washed whatever style her shoulder length honey blonde hair had been cut to and it hung wetly about her face. Her long black coat billowed about her in the sharp intermittent gusts of wind buffeting the cliff tops. The woman's mind was too far away to notice her approach and she gave a start when she noticed the dark-haired girl at her side.

"What's your name?" She asked, pulling her headphones out and letting them dangle from her hand.

The woman stared at her for a while. Her eyes were a dark olive green tarnished by the red puffy skin surrounding them.

"You don't look like a chaplain?"

"I'm not," she held out her hand, "I'm Moira."

The woman continued to stare at her, before giving it a perfunctory squeeze, her nails were painted silver, but the polish was chipped and old. She had the air of a well-groomed woman who'd recently decided it just wasn't worth the effort anymore.

"Tara," she replied, her voice was clipped, precise. Educated, good job, probably financially comfortable.

"You're thinking about jumping, aren't you?" Moira swung her headphones gently back and forth in front of her.

"Of course not."

Moira smiled, "You're not really dressed for hiking..."

She glanced down at the Louboutin heels Tara was wearing.

"Just... needed some air."

"Has it freshened you up?"

Tara flicked at a long strand of damp hair stuck to her face, "A little."

"You're still thinking of jumping, though," Moira insisted.

"You must be some kind of do-gooder. Do you want to talk to me about God?"

"There are no gods, Tara."

"A cult of some kind?"

202

"I like punk rock – does that count?"

"A bit before your time. Aren't kids today all into…" she shrugged "…that stuff that sounds like a car alarm going off?"

"I'm older than I look."

Tara gave a little snort, "Yeah, tell me your secret."

"I will. If you tell me yours."

"I don't have any secrets."

"Why are you here Tara? On the edge of a cliff, soaking wet and dressed like a city businesswoman?"

"I am a city businesswoman."

"Am…" Moira stuffed her headphones into her scuffed leather jacket "…or were?"

Tara raised her chin and focussed on something out to sea. Or maybe nothing at all.

"They let me go a few days ago."

"Ah…"

She looked sharply at her, "I'm not here because of that."

"Taking the air?"

Tara snorted in a breath and wrapped her arms around herself, clutching at the rippling fabric of her expensive and impractical coat.

"My son died. Ten years old. Hit by some drunken fuckwit. Instant. Didn't suffer they said…"

"I'm sorry."

"Everybody is. Even the drunken fuckwit who killed him, he was really sorry. Cried in the dock. Three years he got. Three fucking years. Out in eighteen months, which was longer than my marriage lasted… I don't suppose you smoke?"

Moira shook her head, "Never have."

"Clean living punk?"

Moira shrugged.

"I quit. Several times..." she chewed on her bottom lip, "...feel like starting again."

Moira looked down at the waves pounding the broken, jagged rocks far below them, "There are worse habits..."

"I've... what's the term? Fallen apart," she followed Moira's gaze to the rocks below, "...not sure what's left."

"Why did you get sacked?"

"I developed a taste for shouting at people... to go along with my habit of drinking too much and sleeping with men in the office. I think in the end I wanted to see how far I could go before they would sack me. Poor Tara... you heard about her son? And her marriage? We'll give her a bit more slack. She'll pull through..."

"You will, in the end."

Tara's lips tightened and she shook her head violently enough to set the rat tails of her hair bouncing, "I decided I didn't want to. Screwed up a big job. Lots of money. Which is all that matters to them in the end. When you realise that it doesn't actually matter at all... well, then the world starts looking different."

"The world is different. There's much more to it you know?"

"So much to live for, huh? Not sure I buy that anymore. Nothing seems worth it when you have nothing left."

"There's another world out there, you only have to find it."

Tara ran her fingers through her wet hair and pushed it back out of her face. She closed her eyes, the lids smeared with remnants of purple eyeshadow.

"You're just full of shit and wisdom, aren't you? What the fuck do you know? You're just a kid. Have you lost anyone? Do you know what it actually feels like?"

Moira was silent for a while. Remembering.

"Yes, I've lost someone. A few months ago, actually. Someone I loved..."

"Run off with your best friend, did he? I remember teenage angst."

Moira sometimes wondered why she did what she did.

"No... he died in my arms."

Tara didn't open her eyes, "At least you had a chance to say goodbye."

"The one benefit of dying slowly..."

Moira thought of Jack then, though she'd been trying not to. In the House of Shells with Kalla and her, waiting for the end to come, his frail, bony hand wrapped around hers, half-blind eyes staying with her till the end. Eyes that had always brimmed with love, eyes that had gazed upon her face as if it were a wonder, eyes that had seen the magic of the Fey. Eyes that were now dark and gone.

Thirty-five years they had lived in the House of Shells, and every moment had been blessed. He had wrapped her in his love and she had shown him all the wonders of the Weave, taking his hand and leading him through the ways and paths, the strings and knots. Those eyes had seen giant sea-reeves skimming over waves breaking against a diamond shore, the Endless Spires rising till they pierced the clouds, the Montaine Lakes whose colours changed each day, the Pastel Mountains and the Hills of Mourne, the Singing Caverns and the Grey Forests of the Halladoon. She had shown him all the magic of The Fey.

She had shown him so many things and he had laughed and smiled and gasped and stared in disbelief at them in turn, and yet, despite everything she'd shown him, those eyes of his had always looked at her as if she were the greatest wonder of them all.

But now he was gone. The wraiths had sung their strange haunting laments beneath the light of a million scattered stars and cried tears of sand as she'd buried him beneath the dunes, returning his remains to the weave of the world with only Kalla at her side to share her grief like the spirit-girl always had.

And then she'd been free of her promise to the sand-wraiths, free to go back to the Real and do what she always did. Look for lost souls and try to save them. Such short little lives they suffered here, precious and bright, but fleeting all the same. She stared at Tara.

And some wanted to cut them shorter still.

She could see the disconnect in her, a flicker and a shimmer out of the corner of her eye, just like she had with Jack when their paths had first crossed as they'd sheltered from the rain in a bookshop all those short years ago. A man who'd become lost from the world without even realising it, wrapped in a cloak of sadness he could not see but that was suffocating him all the same.

Sometimes she could save people like Tara and show them a better world. Sometimes it didn't work. Some people could never be saved. And sometimes, just once in a little while, she fell in love with one.

Like Jack. And Harry before him, whose faded photograph still hung in Kalla's care in the House of Shells.

Moira found Tara's hand and entwined her fingers. The woman stiffened but didn't jerk away.

"Come with me," Moira said, giving her a little tug.

"Why would I do that?

"Because there really is a world full of wonders out there..." Moira took a step back from the edge of the cliff "...why don't you let me show it to you..."

# Author's Note

Sometimes you start out on a journey and end up somewhere totally unexpected. With me that usually involves leaving the house to buy groceries and ending up in the pub watching football. I'm sure you know how it is…

After I finish the first draft of a novel I put it aside for three months before starting to edit and rework it, losing familiarity helps focus and allows you to see more clearly what you've actually written as opposed to what you think you've written. That's the theory anyway.

After finishing the first draft of Dark Carnival, rather than twiddle my thumbs for three months I thought I'd try my hand at a short story, something straightforward and more linear than the multi-book epics I've turned in before. A simple horror story about a couple visiting a deserted beach which wouldn't amount to more than 5,000 words and would involve a somewhat sticky end for the adulterous "hero."

Whilst The House of Shells is short by my standards, I overshot my target by a factor of ten and ended up with something entirely different. Ho hum.

I've been deliberately vague about some of the aspects of The House of Shells; particularly Moira, Kalla and The Fey itself. I don't have any immediate plans to return to their story, but you never quite know. A blank page (or a blinking cursor on a pristine screen) can take you to the strangest places and sometimes entirely different ones to those that you intended...

Finally, if you enjoyed *The House of Shells* I'd really appreciate you rating the book or leaving a brief review on the Amazon website. As well as helping a book to sell they make the whole writing experience that little bit more worthwhile to know someone out there has enjoyed my writing.

By Andy Monk

In the Absence of Light

——

*The King of the Winter*

*A Bad Man's Song*

*Ghosts in the Blood*

*The Love of Monsters*

Hawker's Drift

——

*The Burden of Souls*

*Dark Carnival*

Other Fiction

——

*The House of Shells*

# The King of the Winter

After twenty years the road has brought Caleb Cade home.

Running from a broken heart and the hangman's noose he followed it across Europe; searching for happiness in a pretty girl's smile, the turn of a card and the depths of a brandy glass. Instead, he became a womaniser, and then a thief living behind a charmer's mask until, finally, the road ensnared him in insanity and murder.

It is 1708, the Age of The Enlightenment, and, in the shadow of the nearly completed St Paul's Cathedral, Caleb Cade has returned to London a broken man; incapable of love and terrified of the grave, his only friend the half imagined ghost of his brother.

The road has now brought him home for there is nowhere left to run, and his only hope of redemption is to find the man he might have been.

Haunted by his own ghosts and demons, he relives the events of his childhood that led to the death of the only friend he had ever known, and the fear that the King of the Winter is forever peering through the window, all cold of heart and sly of eye, waiting to take him down to damnation.

But whilst one journey ends and another begins. He is befriended by a fellow libertine, Louis Defane, a strange little man around which strange things seem to happen. A man with an insatiable appetite for all the pleasures of life, a man who can seemingly bend people's will to his own, a man with sparkling blue January eyes and snow white hair.

A man who might not be a man at all...

# The Burden of Souls

Small Town, Dark Heart...

...a long ways from anywhere, on a road going nowhere, sits a town surrounded by a sea of grass and vast, turbulent skies. It's a peaceable, prosperous little place in a world that is slowly falling apart, a town where all kinds of people find themselves washed up.

Molly McCrea thinks the husband she never loved was murdered and now there are plans for her. Amos the gunslinger has spent thirteen years searching for a man he knows he'll never find. Preacher Stone is dying, but does the little black bottle that takes the pain away offer something even worse than death? Sam Shenan wants to retire, grow pumpkins and watch the clouds sail by, but thirty years ago he sold his friend for a gold star and a deal is a deal. Guy Furnedge married his wife for her money, but he didn't bargain on her becoming a tormented, bitter alcoholic and now he wants his due. John X Smith sells guns and steals hearts, but is he the only one who knows that the monsters are real? Mr Wizzle sleeps out on the grass hoping to see angels but finds an old friend he's never met instead. Cece Jones arrives bone dry in a rainstorm and sings haunting songs that nobody knows.

All will be drawn into the web weaved through the lives of the town's inhabitants by its urbane and mysterious Mayor; a man prepared to make a deal for your heart's desire, and, maybe, for your very soul...

Further information about Andy Monk's writing and future releases can be found at the following sites:

www.andymonkbooks.com

www.facebook.com/andymonkbooks

Printed in Great Britain
by Amazon

72104531R00130